Storylandia

The Wapshott Journal of Fiction

Issue 26

The Wapshott Press

Storylandia, Issue 26, The Wapshott Journal of Fiction, ISSN 1947-5349, ISBN 978-1-942007-20-3 is published at intervals by the Wapshott Press, now a 501(c)(3) nonprofit, PO Box 31513, Los Angeles, California, 90031-0513, telephone 323-201-7147. All correspondence can be sent to The Wapshott Press, PO Box 31513, LA CA 90031-0513. Visit our website at www.WapshottPress.org to learn more. This work is copyright © 2018 by Storylandia. The Wapshott Journal of Fiction, Los Angeles, California. Copyright © 2017 Tad Bartlett and is reprinted here with the copyright owner's permission.

Storylandia is always seeking quality original short stories, novelettes, and novellas. Please have a look at our submission guidelines at www.Storylandia.WapshottPress.org or email the editor at editor@wapshottpress.org

Cover: "Selma, past midnight, July 2017" by Tad Bartlett, https://wp.me/P1NwPI-A

Storylandia

The Wapshott Journal of Fiction

Founded in 2009

Issue 26, Summer 2018

Edited by Ginger Mayerson

Marchers' Season

By Tad Bartlett

Marchers' Season

by
Tad Bartlett

Marchers' Season

GRAY ALSOBROOK heard muffled voices outside his bedroom window. Car doors slammed and a boy yelled out "Fucker!" and he was awake. Tires screeched and the voices faded away. Gray sat up at the edge of his bed. Doreen snored behind him.

Gray's knees popped and creaked as he stood. He shuffled across the carpet to the window, a draft of cold January air coming in through a crack. Familiar pain shot up his leg. In the shifting shadows of his front yard, long white tails of toilet paper hung from limbs of pine and oak. When their two daughters had been in high school, there'd been half-hearted attempts to roll the trees in the yard, followed by sheepish boys with their "yes, sir" and "sorry, sir." His daughters were gone now—Lilah newly married in Birmingham and Ruthie on an extended path through the university in Tuscaloosa—so this time it was probably aimed at their youngest, Joe.

Gray admired the scope of the job. There was real commitment in it, not a single tree ignored.

The hinges on the front door squeaked. Gray made his way down the hall to find the door ajar. Joe sat on the front steps, looking out at the yard, chin cupped in one hand, his other hand drooped in front of him.

Joe would leave for college in the fall, but lately whenever Gray looked at him, he saw Joe as he looked at ten, only barely still a child. Gray still understood Joe at ten, but now he was a stranger to him. He was tall and scrawny and had let his hair go long. Too long, thought Gray. Joe only seemed to come to life when a friend was over playing basketball at the backyard hoop Gray had set into a plug of concrete when Joe was twelve, or sometimes when Joe was running out the door on a Friday or Saturday night to go to the game or hang out with friends. He made good grades, though, and never came home smelling of cheap alcohol or cigarettes the way Gray had when he was a teenager. Gray figured he shouldn't complain, except for the feeling he'd missed his chance somewhere along the way.

"Joe," Gray said, almost in a grumble

Joe didn't startle or flinch. "Daddy," he said.

"Know who did this? One of your friends?"

"No, sir. None of my friends would do it. Don't matter. I'll clean it up in the morning." He still didn't look back at Gray.

"All right," Gray said. "Use the ladder from round back if you need it."

Joe turned. "Want to help me with it?" he asked.

Gray wanted to tell Joe he would. Wanted to be out in the brisk morning cold with him, doing something together, even if it was just fishing toilet paper out of trees. "I can't, Joe. Going in to the mill in the morning. You'll have it cleaned up before I get home."

Joe looked for a second like he would question Gray about going in on a Saturday. Gray would tell him about the three log skidders and the busted up pickup that were in the equipment and machine shop he supervised, that they had to be back in the woods or on the road by Monday, about how he had men relying on him to be there and a company relying on them to get things fixed. But Joe dropped his eyes and didn't ask.

Instead, Joe stood and slipped in the door, keeping a hand behind him. He brushed past Gray and into the kitchen. He dropped something into the trash can before he turned and said, "'Night, Daddy." As Joe passed, he gave Gray a little slap on his arm, what went for a hug anymore, then walked down the hall toward his bedroom.

"G'night, son," Gray said. When Joe's door clicked shut, Gray walked into the kitchen and pulled a crumpled sheet of paper off the top of the trash. He turned it over. Scrawled in red was a hangman drawing like the kids used to make when playing word games on family car trips. On eleven dashed lines under the drawing were the all-capped letters, N̲ I G̲ G̲ E̲ R̲ L O̲ V̲ E R̲.

Gray could feel his pulse pound in his temples. This kind of thing, still, in 1990. He felt dizzy as he walked to Joe's door. He wanted to find out who did this, ask Joe what it was for or why he hadn't shown it to him. But when he raised his fist to knock on Joe's door, he stopped. He dropped his hand to the doorknob, but paused again without turning it. He would talk to Doreen about it in the morning. Together they could figure it out.

He folded the paper neatly and walked back into his room.

WHEN GRAY finished breakfast, Joe was still asleep. Gray pulled on his steel-toed boots and went out the front door to his company truck, all white except for the red corporate logo of the Canadian paper company that had bought the mill fifteen years before. Toilet paper fluttered in the fragile light.

It was early yet, only six, but the mill was an hour's drive away over Alabama back-country roads. He turned on the radio as he pulled out of the driveway. The fishing and hunting report would come on soon. Maybe the next weekend things would have calmed down enough in the shop so he could head out in the woods before deer season was over.

A news reporter launched into a story. "In the wake of Wednesday's school board vote to not renew the contract of the school system's first African-American superintendent, Russell Livaudais, approximately fifty students gathered on the front steps of Meadowview High School yesterday afternoon. They blocked the line of cars waiting to pick up children after school. Many held signs, saying 'No Justice, No Peace,' and 'Keep Racism Out of Our Schools.'"

Gray snorted. The board's six white members had voted against renewing Livaudais's contract, and the five black ones had voted for the renewal. There'd been a community meeting the next night— something about "Save Our Schools"—and the stories in the paper quoted the usual agitators talking about racism in the government, but Gray always figured there was more to the story.

A woman's voice came on in the report. "Is this what they're teaching our kids? Instigate trouble and block innocent children from getting to their parents?"

The news reporter came back in. "Those were parent Linda Maples' questions, as she was caught up in the protest outside the school. One of the few white students standing in the blockade, senior Joe Alsobrook, had this to say in response..."

Gray looked at the radio, as if he would see

his son's face there. He turned up the volume. Joe's voice, older than he ever imagined, came through the speakers. "We all grew up together. If we've learned something, it's that color doesn't– shouldn't– matter. Doctor Livaudais is a good superintendent. He comes around our classes. He knows all of us, by name. He cares about us. It's the Board, now, that's taught us a different kind of lesson. Our town needs to do better, to be better. We, the students, need to be heard."

When the story was over, Gray grabbed a pack of cigarettes from the console and lit one, then cranked down his window a crack. Cold wind roared in his ear. Joe sometimes brought black friends to the house to shoot baskets or study, but none of them ever seemed the angry, protesting kind. The two-lane in front of Gray was empty of cars, and Gray looked off the roadside at the sunlight cutting through the trees. He tried to picture Joe standing at the head of a pack of students, talking to reporters, facing down angry mothers, but he couldn't. Joe wasn't so serious as that. He was just a kid.

Three deer, a large buck with an eight-point rack and two does, stepped out from the roadside brush and froze on the shoulder, staring down his truck. Gray swerved, said a small prayer they wouldn't jump out at him. They didn't.

The pickup truck waiting for him in the equipment shop had a caved-in grill and smashed radiator from one of the dumb beasts. The deer had flipped up over the hood and crashed through the windshield. The pickup driver had been taken by ambulance to the little hospital in Grove Hill. He'd come back with a bandage covering one eye and a stitched gash down his cheek from a deer hoof, a splint taped to his nose, and his arm in a sling. He'd said the deer had mauled him in its scramble to get out of the cab, then shook its head after it was out, jumped a guardrail by the side of the road, and tore off into the trees. Gray had heard similar stories a handful of times, as deer looking for easy forage along roadsides would smash up cars, almost always giving worse than they got.

Gray watched in his rearview as the three deer slowly walked across the road. He rounded a curve and they were gone.

WHEN GRAY was little, all the grown-ups around their small Arkansas town called him "Little Joe." His dad, Joseph Gray Alsobrook, Jr., was "Big Joe." Big Joe had a red face, big arms, and flat gray eyes. Gray remembered the sound of a big laugh, but only through a wall or from down a hall. With Gray, Big Joe was almost wordless, grim, a belt-wielder when Gray brought home a bad note from the teacher, a doler out of Saturday chores before he headed into town "for supplies."

The most Big Joe ever said to Gray at one time was the morning after Gray's tenth birthday. It was a Monday morning in October.

Gray was in the front yard, pushing his new bike through the yard to ride to school. It had been a birthday present the day before. It was a 1952 Schwinn Hornet, bright metallic green, with the rack on the back and a fender light on the front. Gray had been eyeing it for months, and couldn't believe his luck.

Big Joe hustled out the front door. "Hold up, Little Joe," he said. Gray stopped and looked at his dad, not sure what he'd done.

"Yessir?" he asked.

"Let me take that," Big Joe said, grabbing the

top bar of the bike and wheeling it toward his pickup. "Come on," he said, "I'll drive you to school." Big Joe never drove Gray to school. Gray rarely ever saw him on weekday mornings at all, with Big Joe usually up and gone to his construction job before Gray ever woke up, and that was on the mornings when Big Joe wasn't sleeping over in whatever little town he was working in.

Big Joe lifted the bike over the tailgate. Gray hoisted himself up into the cab and slammed the door behind him.

"Whatcha' think, boy, 'bout being ten?" Big Joe asked as they bounced over the dirt ruts of the lane they lived on.

"It's all right, sir," Gray said. "I like it good enough."

Big Joe glanced at Gray, then stared back in front of him. "Good enough," he repeated after a moment. "Good enough. Yeah, well I guess that's about the song of it," he said.

The two of them rode in silence for a couple minutes, until Big Joe reached the end of the lane and turned out onto the black top of the county road. From there it was another mile into town.

"Where you working at this week, Daddy?" Gray asked.

Big Joe looked over at Gray. "Huh," he said. "I don't know. Maybe Montana, I'm thinking. Or California."

"How's that?" Gray asked. "They're a long way from Arkansas." Big Joe was usually working all over the little hill towns of northern Arkansas, sometimes even as far away as Little Rock or occasionally up into Missouri. One time he had a job in Memphis and was gone from home for three months.

"Don't question me, boy," Big Joe said softly, not harsh like he usually said those words. He pulled the truck over into the weeds beside the road. In the distance, Gray could see the brick school buildings at the edge of town.

"Why we stopping?" Gray asked.

Big Joe turned and faced him. "It's time you stopped being called Little Joe," he said. "You're just Joe now."

"What do you mean, sir?" Gray asked.

"You need to be a man now, son." Big Joe wrenched the door handle and got out of the cab, but didn't close the door behind him.

"Come on, Joe," he said, "climb across." Gray slid across the bench seat and climbed down. Big Joe put a foot up on the running board and leaned down eye level with Gray. "Joe," he said, "I've got to leave."

"What, Daddy?" Gray said. "Why? How long'll you be gone?" He had to squint at Big Joe, because the morning sun was shining down over Big Joe's shoulder and straight into Gray's face.

"Look, I've given my time to you, and we ain't going to pussyfoot around this. My daddy only stuck around till I was three," Big Joe said.

"What're you talking about?" Gray asked.

Big Joe straightened up, throwing Gray's face back in shadow. "You'll understand when you're growed up, Joe. Alsobrook men, we don't root down. We ain't trees. We're rivers. My daddy went off. His daddy, the first Big Joe, hell, he didn't even stick to see my daddy get born." Big Joe leaned back against the seat, and the sun shined back down into Gray's eyes.

"You ain't leaving," he yelled at Big Joe. "You ain't leaving!"

Big Joe balled a hand into a fist and looked down at his boots. Then he slid backward onto his seat, loosened his fist and reached out to put his hand on Gray's head. "You'll run, too, one day, Joe. Then you'll understand. We're like rivers." His hand fell from Gray's head and reached out to the door handle. "Now, get on to school. And when you get home, you be strong for your Mama. You're the Joe in the house now." And then Big Joe slammed the door shut.

The red pickup started to roll up onto the pavement, its rounded fenders smooth like a greased pig. Gray yelled out, "Hey!" The pickup stopped, half up onto the roadway. "Hey," Gray yelled again. Big Joe rolled his window down, scowled out at Gray.

"What is it, boy?" he asked.

"I ain't your Joe," Gray said. "I ain't no one's Joe. Not Little Joe, not Big Joe, not no kind of Joe. I ain't taking your damn name. I'm Gray," he said. "Gray Alsobrook."

Big Joe's scowl turned into momentary puzzlement, then he looked away, through the windshield in front of him. Gray saw him pump his neck, like he was cussing. Then the pickup rolled onto the pavement and took off down the road. Gray Alsobrook stood on the roadside, alone, angry, without his bike. He kicked a pebble, then walked the rest of the way into town.

GRAY PULLED the company truck into the front gravel lot closest to the mill administration building. A couple other company trucks, belonging to other managers, were in the lot. The back gravel lot farthest from the building was dotted with the pickup trucks of the weekend crews. In the administration building, the receptionist's wood paneled alcove was empty.

Gray passed by the time clock used by the hourly employees and out the back door, where he cut left behind the main boiler building and toward the equipment yard and shop.

As he walked through the large open garage door into the shop, he called out, "Yo," to Cyrus, his foreman, who stretched over the engine of the deer-damaged pickup truck. The crinkled hood lay on the concrete floor. A new one leaned on a pallet against a wall. Cyrus was the first black foreman in the shop, the first promotion Gray had made when he was elevated from foreman to supervisor. Cyrus had been in the shop longer than anyone in the time that Gray had been there, so when Lon, the old supervisor, retired and Gray was promoted, it just made sense. He heard a year later, during the renewal negotiations with the union, that the white union leadership were raising a stink over black folks starting to get promoted over the whites. He was called into one of the VP's offices in the admin building and asked whether he'd create a new position above foreman, an assistant supervisor, to put one of the young white union bucks into.

"Don't need an 'assistant supervisor,' Harold," Gray had told the earnest-faced Canadian executive.

"I know you don't, Gray. It's what I told them, that you don't need one and you wouldn't go for it. But the union's holding it over us," Harold had said.

"Cause I got a damn black foreman in my shop? Hell, Cyrus has been at this mill thirty damn years. Best mechanic in the place."

Harold had held both hands up to Gray. "Don't go getting agitated now. I know it isn't right, and I'm not going to make you do it. Heck, Gray."

"Well?" Gray had said.

"OK, then," Harold had replied. "Leave it be."

Not long after that, every white employee in the shop had transferred out to other parts of the mill. Gray was fine with that.

"Good Saturday, Mr. Gray," Cyrus called back to Gray as he made his way to his little office walled off in one corner of the shop. Willie and Tom, two other mechanics, were under one of the skidders. All three of them were getting time and a half, as well as a day off from their wives. Gray smiled at the nude Miss January on the calendar on the wall outside his office door, before squeezing through the door and around his metal desk and into the creaking green leather of the second-hand desk chair. Even three years after Lon's retirement, the office still smelled of the old man's cheap cigars. It was familiar. Sometimes he thought that maybe old Big Joe must've smoked cigars in addition to his pipes. Cheap cigars and pipe smoke equals fathers. Stove-burned milk equals mothers.

As Gray looked over the stack of invoices on his desk, wondering where he should start, Cyrus poked his head through the door.

"Hey, boss, just the three on top are new. Sign those and I'll stick 'em back in the mill post," Cyrus said.

Gray picked up a pen from the desk, and straightened the stack of invoices. "Thanks. Then I'll give you a hand with that truck?"

"If you want to, but I got it. You salaried folks ain't getting no extra pay on a Saturday." Cyrus grinned. This was an old pact. Cyrus knew he'd never shake Gray on an off-day when there were heavy machines in the shop that needed to be out in the woods. Gray knew every man in there would rather be sitting by a stream somewhere, or in a deer stand, or flushing turkeys out into a field. Or visiting the sex woman the next town over, around the next bend, on the way out "for a pack of cigarettes, be right back." The mill generally let Gray and his shop run on its own, no interference from the higher corporate dictates, but in exchange Gray took care of his men, and made sure the mill's equipment was never out of commission for long.

When Gray got back over to the pickup Cyrus was working on, Cyrus had the grill off and had lowered the new radiator into place. While Cyrus was tightening the nuts on the radiator bracket, Gray leaned down to look at the grill.

"Didn't see an invoice for a new grill," he said. "Think we can bang this thing back straight?"

"Sure," Cyrus said between grunts as he torqued the last nut into place. "Just bent one way. Got a mallet that'll take care of that."

"Yeah," Gray said. He picked up the grill and carried it over to a large table under a window at the front of the shop. He picked out a heavy rubber-headed mallet and began to steadily beat the grill back into shape. It wasn't going to be showroom ready, but nobody in the woods or on the backroads would care much about that. It would do the job, let air through and keep the brush and rocks out.

As he walked it back over to the truck, Cyrus was standing back to look at the radiator, wiping the grease off his hands with a shop rag he always kept stuffed into his back pocket. Willie and Tom leaned against the side of the truck.

"This do?" Gray asked as he handed the grill back to Cyrus. He knew it would more than do, but he liked his guys to see him work, and work well.

"Yeah, boss. That's all right," Cyrus said, looking at the grill before leaning it against the front of the truck. "Break for some coffee?"

They walked over to the folding table outside Gray's office, where a coffeemaker sat, guarded over by the nudie calendar. They sat on some folding chairs by the table, steaming styrofoam cups of coffee in hand.

Tom looked up at the calendar. "She pretty enough," he said, "but ain't no March."

"Ain't nobody gonna be like March," Willie said, and they all laughed, even Gray. After Lon had retired and the next year turned over, he hadn't put up the new calendar from the engine supplier, not right away. But the men had complained enough times that Gray put it up and didn't blink about it again.

"But June sure was nice, too," Gray said. The other men smiled at him, then looked back at January.

"You don't got to say that, you know," Willie said.

"What? I mean it."

"Now, you a white man who likes his chocolate, then, that's all right," Tom said, and laughed again. June had been the only black calendar girl that year. There was always one.

"Just women, Tom. Ain't no problems with that," Gray said. He wished he'd just kept his mouth shut. Sometimes it wasn't worth trying to talk.

"That's right," Cyrus said. "That's right." He'd been quiet, laughing a little softer and a little less, sipping his coffee, concentrating on the floor. Then he said, "Tell me something, Mr. Gray, your son still in school?"

"Sure. Though not for long. Graduating this spring." The pictures in his office were ten years old, the kids young and looking like angels in wide lapels.

"His name Joe?" Cyrus asked.

Gray felt uneasy. "You heard that radio news this morning?"

Cyrus nodded. Willie and Tom looked up at Miss January some more, pretending they weren't listening.

"Yeah," Gray said, "well I don't really know much about what's going on up there, you know, at the school."

"Well he sounded real grown up, Mr. Gray. You doing good," Cyrus said.

Gray sipped more at his coffee cup, though there was nothing else in it, then looked up at Cyrus. He nodded his head, grunted. Then the four men stood and walked over to look at the skidders.

ON GRAY'S thirteenth birthday, he was determined to become a man.

A couple months before, Gray had been crawling in the cool dark under the raised house, waiting to ambush the lead battalion of the Chinese Red Army in the DMZ, when behind a brick pier he'd found Big Joe's left-behind stash of tobacco pipes, a metal flask of something that made Gray's eyes sting when he unscrewed the lid to sniff it, and a blue tin of Kentucky Club. *The thoroughbred of pipe tobaccos,* read the faded label.

On his birthday, after the birthday cake candles had been blown out, the cake eaten, and all his friends but Tim had gotten back on their bikes and pedaled back down the driveway toward their homes, Gray kissed his mom on her cheek, said "thank you, ma'am," and headed with Tim out the back screen door and into the woods that closed up on the backyard.

"So what's back in here," Tim asked as the two boys whacked at vines and branches with a couple sticks, like jungle explorers with machetes through thick undergrowth.

"You'll see," Gray said, trying to pitch his voice deeper. "It'll put hair on your chest, though, I guarantee that." Gray hoped it was true.

"What's it? A girl?" Tim laughed. Gray let a branch slap back into Tim. "Ow!"

"Naw, it ain't no girl. It's something men do and don't have to worry about no girls."

"I don't want to get in trouble," Tim said. "Besides, you ain't no man yet."

Gray stopped in a clearing just big enough for the sun to reach down to the spot of ground where he stood. He turned and faced Tim. Gray felt the ugliness that welled up when he needed to push tears and lip-trembles down.

"I am, too, a man," Gray said, working to control his words. "My daddy says the Jews treat their boys like men when they turn thirteen. And he says we're better than them Jews anyway." Then he spat on the ground to the side of Tim's feet. "You a sissy, Tim Butler, or are you a man?"

Tim's face grew calm. "Boy, don't talk to me about no Jews. Like you even know any. I been thirteen a lot longer than you. And your daddy's done left you anyhow. What, three years? Shit."

"Ain't true," Gray said. "He's off in Korea, fighting. That's all. He'll be back."

"Boy, knock it off. I heard my mama telling about how your daddy left you and your mom, up and left, how he's no-good trash. And there ain't no more Korea. That war been done with now a long time."

Gray wanted two things. He wanted to tell Tim he was right and apologize to him so he could have a friend he didn't have to lie to, so he could have someone who knew his secret and didn't care. But he also wanted to punch Tim Butler right in his mouth, make his lips bust open and bleed down his shirt, pop his teeth out, make him cry. Not only couldn't he do both, but he realized he couldn't do either.

"Go home," he said to Tim. "Just go on home. I don't want you out in these woods."

Tim looked at Gray for a long moment, then he shook his head, turned, dropped his stick, and walked back out of the woods.

When Gray couldn't hear Tim's footsteps shuffling through the leaves any longer, he kneeled down in the center of the clearing and pried up a large rock he'd been standing on. Underneath, in a hollow he'd dug and scraped out with his pocket knife, was a rolled-up, dirty canvas sack. When he unrolled the sack, the flask, one of the pipes—a red wood, maybe cherry—and the blue tin of tobacco tumbled out onto the ground.

Gray popped open the tin, pinched out a wad of dried up tobacco, and smushed it down into the bowl of the pipe. He dug a book of matches out of his pants pocket, struck one, and held it down into the pipe while he sucked in on the stem. Immediately, his head swam in circles. He felt like he couldn't breathe. He coughed out a cloud of smoke and then couldn't draw in enough breath to cough again. He sipped in air as he bent down to the ground. He dropped the pipe so he could hold onto the dirt with both hands. When he finally had air back in his lungs and caught his breath, his stomach began to turn.

He eyed the flask, still lying on the ground. He grabbed it and twisted off the cap. Without stopping to smell it, he put it up to his mouth and turned his face to the sky, the liquid burning across his tongue to the back of his throat. As soon as he swallowed it, though, he felt it all coming back up. The smoke, the alcohol, the cake, the barbecue he'd had for his birthday lunch. And it did, all over the pattern of leaves on the forest floor. White icing, bits of yellow cake, strips of sauce-lacquered meat, red like blood, then endless bile, yellow, green, then just clear strands of spit as his stomach kept rebelling even after it was empty.

When Gray's body quieted, his breathing eased, and he stood up. The daylight was almost gone. He reached down and put the flask and the pipe back in the sack. He rolled it up. He hefted it in his hand. He was calm. He cocked his arm back, and threw the sack as deep into the woods as he could.

ON SUNDAY mornings, Gray had a regular coffee-and-grousing session with a group of silver-haired bastards. He was a good ten years younger than most of the other men at the formica-topped table at the Downtown Pancake House—*Nothing International About It*, proclaimed the menus—but they seemed to enjoy his company. Made them feel younger, he figured. They would all drink bad coffee and some would eat runny eggs and runnier grits, and they'd trade insults and lies and complaints about their wives, and pass over the events of the week. Then they'd drive off to their various churches to meet their families for eleven o'clock service.

"My boy Will and I got us a six-pointer yesterday morning," Bill Youngblood said, after a loud slurp from his coffee. "He had his oldest boy with us. Eight years old. His first time."

There was a chorus around the table of "good for him," and "six points ain't bad, but ain't eight," and "when you going to bring me some venison sausage," before Blaine Cranston, who used to own the mill and all the land around it before he sold it to the Canadians, waved his hands at the table and said, "So what'd the boy think, the young 'un?"

"He was wide-eyed, you know," Bill said.

"That's the critical time right there," Blaine said, "where you grip him up and show him the way things work. What'd y'all do?"

"Well, we made him walk out in front of us, lead us to where the buck fell. When we got there, the buck was still strugglin', you know. Will's boy looked up at us. Wasn't sure whether he was going to cry or something. I gave him my hunting knife, and Will lay across the buck and showed the boy how to slice cross the jugular." Bill stopped, raised bushy eyebrows across the table at Blaine.

Gray broke in. "Did he do it?"

"Course he did. His first kill. Drank the blood and everything. We smeared it on his cheeks, made him look like a little wild man. His mama was mortified when we got him home, but I was proud of that boy," Bill said.

Joe and Gray hadn't hunted together in a long time. Joe had begged off the last couple seasons, and Gray hadn't pushed the issue much. Gray liked the woods alone.

The waitress, Glinda, an older black woman who had worked there ever since Gray could remember and likely long before that, came around the table and topped off coffee mugs, and the hubbub of the men settled down. "Get y'all anything else this morning?" she asked.

"Naw, Glinda, we're all good here," Blaine said, putting a business smile on. "Thank you, girl."

"All right, then," Glinda said, her smile thin and pasted on.

Blaine watched her walk away, then turned back toward the table of men, leaning in a bit. "So y'all see what them jungle monkeys all up to at the school?"

Gray's stomach churned, and he looked to see if Glinda showed any sign of hearing, then he returned Blaine's stare. The other men chuckled low until Jimbo Smitherman, red-faced, said, "Always getting up about something, them people. Now their kids're getting in on the act."

"Yeah," Bill joined in, looking over his shoulder before adding, "Ain't nobody saying a word about how them nigger board members all voted together, too. How come they ain't being called out?"

"Don't work that way," Jimbo said. "You know that. We all know that."

"What you think, Gray?" Blaine asked. "I heard they're going to march on the Board of Education building after school one day this week. Stop traffic and everything."

Gray wanted to leave it be, but Blaine's question had everyone looking at him. He wondered if they'd all caught on that his son was in on the protests.

"I haven't heard about that, about the school board building," Gray responded. Blaine always seemed to know things before they happened.

"Well now, I don't know. Maybe it ain't happening," Blaine said, "but I wouldn't be surprised. Always trying to ape it up for the cameras, you know."

Gray took a moment to slurp at his coffee. "Hell, Blaine," he said, "I suppose there's a little bit to what Jimbo says, folks just protesting so they can protest."

"Yeah," Blaine said, turning his gaze down to the formica tabletop for a moment before looking back squarely at Gray. "But these kids, now. They're impressionable. It's bad news."

"Ain't nobody going to stay living around this place," Jimbo interrupted, "if folks keep living in the damn past."

They were all still looking at Gray, though nobody'd yet mentioned Joe. "Well, maybe there's real issues folks should think about," Gray said. "I mean, the protesters, of course," Gray said. "I hear there's reasons the board could've voted the way they did. Like some teachers didn't like Livaudais's management style or something."

"I heard that, too," Blaine said, "or maybe the board just figured out before it was too late that you don't let the animals run the zoo. What do you think about that?"

Gray couldn't figure why Blaine would keep on him so heavy, except that he probably did know about Joe. Not that Blaine ever had to worry about anything with all his land money. His kid would never worry none, either.

"Well," he said, and the old men's eyes stayed on him, "Marching never hurt no one."

"Bullshit," Bill said. "What about after 'Nam? All those troops coming home to them hippies marching in the street, spitting on soldiers in airports. Shit."

"Not that you'd know a damn thing about it," Gray said, "but it sure beat having 'Cong shooting at you all the time." This was Gray's one bit of seniority over the men around the table. They'd all been too old to go to Vietnam and too young for Korea. A lost half-generation of damn war-mongering dilettantes.

Blaine tightened his lips and red creeped up his

cheeks. The conversation had slipped away from him. Glinda came back around to the table and dropped the bill in front of him.

Jimbo turned talk to the weather change coming later in the week. The weatherman had promised an unusual January warm front was going to sweep across from the west coast, pushing the chill out with a posse of storms and a few days of muggy warmth.

Bill sighed, "It's going to confuse all the damned azaleas."

Gray dropped cash on the table for his coffee and left for church.

AFTER CHURCH, Gray and Joe went to work on the piece of bottomland that dropped off on the other side of the driveway, up by the road. Closer to the house, the creek bottom gully was an easy hike through well-spaced and towering trees. Joe had practically lived down there when he was little, coming home with tadpoles and crawfish and snakes that he'd keep in tubs full of muddy water or in cracked-glass old aquariums he'd find god-knows-where, all arranged on the side porch of the house, stinking like sewer and dead things. But closer to the road the bottomland was a tangle of undergrowth and tight-packed saplings. And when the whole creek bottom would fill up with flood every spring or two, any trash that couldn't wash through the culvert under the road—whole trees, tires, discarded furniture, rusted barrels—would catch up in the bramble, too.

Whenever there was a weekend without grass to cut or leaves to rake, Gray would put Joe to work with him clearing it out, hacking at it with axes and saws, little by little clearing it away, then dragging the large piles of it up the steep gully-side to stack by the road.

"Why we gotta do this?" Joe asked that Sunday afternoon.

"I've told you before," Gray answered between swings of his axe. He thwacked at the base of a sugarberry tree, exposing the white pulp inside the gray bark. "Keep the rodents down." Thwack again, the wood splintering at the trunk. "Which keeps the snakes from getting too many." Thwack again, clean through, the little tree jumping down, standing for a moment, then falling to the side.

Truth was, Gray didn't know why he did it, really, clearing the bottom out. Sometimes he dreamed about building a little workshop down there, or something Joe could use as a clubhouse, or that grandkids one day, maybe, could play in. He wasn't going to eradicate all the rodents, or make a dent in the population of snakes running through all this bottomland and up into the backyards of him and his neighbors, not by knocking down one stand of trash trees. It was something for him to do, and maybe more important, for Joe to do. Keep him working, from being spoilt like Blaine's kid. Maybe teach Joe a thing or two, like he never had anyone do for him.

A couple hours every weekend of this, or the lawn mower in spring and summer, or the rake in the fall. Blisters on the hands, bug bites and sweat. It wasn't much.

And maybe, when he and Doreen were old, they'd stick around this town and have a nice place, a pretty piece of property to gaze at. Roots of their own.

When they were done for the afternoon, Gray and Joe stretched out on the sofas in the living room, a John Wayne movie on the television and a bowl of popcorn between them. An hour into it, Joe was asleep. Gray went into the kitchen, where Doreen was polishing the good silverware. It had been jumbled in a pile in a corner of the counter since Christmas dinner a few weeks before, washed but tarnished.

"Hey, hon," Gray said. Doreen looked at him, one strand of her barely graying dark hair escaped from the ponytail holder and running down the side of her face. She smiled at him. His heart lightened. "Was thinking about throwing something on the grill for supper, steaks or something."

"Sounds good," Doreen said.

"Joe's napping on the sofa. Want to ride to the Winn Dixie with me?"

Doreen looked down at the fork in her hand, buffing out the last of the polish. She put it in a stack of shining utensils to her right, then waved her hand over at the diminished pile of silverware still to do. "Sure, Gray. I'll save the rest for later."

"You've been saying that for weeks now," Gray said to her, gently. He didn't want her to think he was telling her what to do. It was more just ribbing than anything, things husbands and wives got away with saying to each other if they'd been friends long enough.

"You're the one who asked me to come," she said. "I can just stay here."

"Naw," Gray said, because he really wanted her with him. Maybe they'd talk. "We can take a drive after, just you and me."

The Winn Dixie was five minutes away, near the western edge of town. Often it was peopled with folks from out in the country, stopping off at the closest real grocery to their farms or their little crossroads collections of houses. But Gray and Doreen would always run into someone they knew from town.

Meadowview was the big town around there, twenty-thousand people, the county seat, but it wasn't so big. Late afternoon on a Sunday, an hour before the store closed, pale winter light coming in through the big plate-glass windows at the front of the store, there were more folks than usual pushing baskets up and down the narrow, linoleum-tiled aisles.

Gray and Doreen browsed over the cuts of beef in the meat case along the back walls of the store. Doreen eyed them for lines of gristle and marbling of fat. Gray hefted them for weight and looked at the "good by" date. Janice Youngblood, Bill's wife, was working her way slowly toward them, pushing a basket and looking at poultry parts. Gray elbowed Doreen and nodded his head toward Janice.

"Hello, Janice," Doreen said, putting that smile in her voice like she did at church or at the kids' school events. Gray liked that Doreen could be the social one, the nice one.

Janice looked up at Doreen and Gray, startled. But instead of replying, she made an audible huff, set her shoulders, and pushed her basket into an adjacent aisle.

"Janice?" Doreen asked, but not to anybody, because Janice was already halfway down the aisle. Doreen stood, holding the steak she'd been examining. "That's weird," she said to Gray.

"You think so?"

"Of course it is, Gray. People in this town don't just snub you like that. It takes too much energy." She looked at Gray. "I hate to say it, but I think it's got to do with Joe."

"Yeah. Probably." Gray was glad she'd brought it up. He hadn't talked to her, yet, about the hangman note he'd found in the trash two nights before. When she'd mentioned the toilet paper in the trees when he came home from the mill on Saturday, he'd just told her that yards get rolled all the time. But he'd had the note folded up in his pocket, next to his wallet, for when they could talk.

They walked toward the checkout lanes with two packs of steaks. Gray felt stares from everyone, though no one was looking their way when he turned. "Fellas at the Pancake House were kind of strange today," he said to Doreen. "They didn't say anything specific about Joe, but they brought up the protesting and were looking at me, expecting something."

"I'm sure they know Joe's involved. It's a small town." They paid for the steaks and walked out to the car, the big Oldsmobile they'd bought a few years before. The sky above them was a deep blue, almost violet, a single contrail stretched across it. The wind out of the north was brisk, though it wasn't otherwise too cold. Not the Arkansas cold Gray grew up with.

Gray steered the car out of the parking lot and headed onto the two-lane roads that wound through the hills rolling outside of town.

"So I found Joe throwing away a note Friday night, when I got up and saw the yard rolled." He slipped the folded paper out of his pocket and handed it over to Doreen, keeping his eyes on the road.

Doreen unfolded it and sighed. "He's just so visible," she said, turning to stare out the window at woods and farmland.

"You think we should worry more about it?" Gray asked.

"I don't know, Gray, I really don't. I know we've always said we can feel at home in this town, that everybody watches out for everybody, but sometimes."

"Ain't anybody lynching anybody around

here, not these days." Gray wanted to not be worried, wanted to trust this town he'd decided would be their town, where they'd raised this family.

"It could be just kids, Gray, getting out their Friday nights on the first person they can think of. It was just toilet paper. You said it, right? Yards get rolled all the time." Doreen carefully folded the hangman note back up.

"I wonder if folks would even notice who was doing the protesting," Gray said, "if it was just black kids." He turned onto a smaller road that would wind them back toward town. "Maybe we should ask him if he shouldn't stop."

Doreen jerked her head toward Gray. "You know that ain't the right answer, Gray Alsobrook."

Gray put his hand over on Doreen's knee. "I know it ain't ideal, but he's so close. So close to getting out of this place. I know we don't mind it here."

"But it's got its flaws, all right," Doreen finished his thought.

"You can see it chafes on him. He ain't ever doing things easy. That girlfriend last fall...." Gray let his sentence trail off. Joe had never said anything, never brought the girl, Amy, around, and it hadn't amounted to anything, but for a couple months there'd been the uneasy whispers about the white boy and the black girl dating at the high school. "... And now this."

The sky was darkening into dusk. Though it wasn't night-dark yet, Gray switched his headlights on. They illuminated a hulk of brown fur heaving on the roadside a hundred feet ahead.

"Pull over, Gray," Doreen said. Gray glided to a stop on the grassy shoulder, the headlights washing over the animal. As Gray and Doreen sat in the car watching, the animal lifted its head. A huge buck with a spreading rack of antlers. It struggled, flopping its legs. As it did so, Gray saw the blood spurt up from its body.

Gray got out, and Doreen opened her door. "Be careful, hon," he said. "It's just as likely to gore you as look at you."

"You hush, Gray. He's too hurt to fight anyone."

And he was. Gray stepped carefully up to the deer. It laid its head back down, watching out of one large, dark, wet eye. The hide over its mid-section was ripped away, and its intestines spilled out onto the grass. A pool of dark red blood spread around it.

"He's magnificent," Gray whispered. He counted the points on the rack in the light from their car headlights. Thirteen.

"Poor thing," Doreen said. "Too bad you don't have your gun with you to put him out of his misery." She knelt down, way too close to that rack of antlers, thought Gray. She put a hand on the deer's neck. "There, there," she said, almost cooing to the thing.

The sky grew darker, and the shadows beneath the trees beside the road lengthened until their blackness reached right up to the edge of the headlight glow. The deer shut his eyes, opened them, then shut them again, leaving them closed. Doreen picked her hand up off his neck and stood.

"He's gone," she said. "Dogs'll get him tonight."

"And the vultures tomorrow," Gray said.

WHEN GRAY came home from his third tour, he was no longer surprised that the stories were myths, that nobody actually spit on him in the airport. Hell, nobody did anything, except maybe make an effort to *not* look at him. It was mid-summer, 1970. They were all as tired of it as he was, he figured, though being tired of things seemed pretty petty for folks on their side of it. He'd seen their marches in pictures in the pages of *Stars and Stripes*. Drums and flowers in downtown streets, angry-smile chants, fists in the air. Gray's march was silent and alone on airport terminal tiles, surrounded by ghosts, at least until he turned a corner and saw Doreen and the girls.

Little Ruthie, five, bounced like a cork on a fishing line, all dark curls and smile. Delilah, seven, stood still, a serious look on a face framed by long, straight, light brown hair parted down the middle like a curtain, as if she were wondering how long this time before her dad went back over there, to a place she knew from the nightly news was trying to kill him, to a place that filled her nightmares. And then there was Doreen, tall, legs, a beige dress cinched in at the waist, gracefully lining out—all of her—in just the right directions and just the right ways from there, every bit the beauty queen he'd fallen for and knocked up while they were both still in college, twenty-one, young and not young. He'd enlisted, the girls had come, one then the other, he'd re-enlisted, and then he was in-country, three times, a year at a time, thirty-days' leave between each, never enough.

Gray and Doreen and the girls spent the next thirty days driving across country, hopping from one national park and roadside attraction to another. He tried not to watch the news when they stopped at diners, or nights in motel rooms. Instead, evenings, hot, distant lightning flashes in the sky, he'd sit outside the motel room door in a folding lawn chair, whiskey in a motel glass tumbler in his hand, Doreen in a chair next to him, his girls cross-legged on the ground at their feet, and he would feel the warm

American breeze on his skin. He would catch Lilah, and sometimes Ruthie, staring up at him, then looking away, then looking back. He knew that feeling, that distrust that dad would be there. He aimed to beat it back, with a small smile here or there, covert, in the rearview mirror or across a diner tabletop. A squeezing of hands on the rim of the Grand Canyon. A sip of beer from an icy mug slid across a wooden table in a cavernous, bayou-side fish camp, and a wink, a don't-tell-your-mother conspiracy.

By the time the thirty days were almost up, and the Alsobrook family was rolling down the last miles into Fayetteville, North Carolina—FayetteNam, home of Fort Bragg—he knew he wasn't going to sign the papers to re-enlist again. He was done.

ON TUESDAY night, the wind roared in the tall trees rising from the creek-bottom, cold. The weather was readying to change, the winter gathering up its skirts ahead of a train of warm, moist air out of the Gulf, a wrinkle of front making a feint north over land, high enough up into Alabama to catch their Black Belt town, maybe then as far north as Birmingham, stretching for Cullman, Huntsville, Nashville, before sweeping back south again and east, past Atlanta and out to sea through Savannah and the long beaches of Tybee Island.

When Gray got home from the mill, it was already dark out. A strange car was in the driveway, probably one of Joe's friends. Gray came in the side door of the house, into the kitchen, and slammed the door against the wind. As he pulled his arms out of his coat and hung it across the back of a kitchen stool, his nose filled with the smell of garlic and charred onion. Doreen was pulling a meatloaf out of the oven.

"Whose car?" Gray asked.

"Shaun's," Doreen answered, raising an eyebrow as she said it. Shaun was from the other side of town, but he and Joe had been best friends since the fifth grade, at least until the previous fall.

"Thought they weren't hanging out any more, after that thing with the girl." Gray crossed the kitchen and put a roughened hand on Doreen's hip. He pulled his face in close to hers.

Doreen let a chuckle escape from her throat. She closed the gap between them with a kiss before pushing him gently away, her hand on his chest. "Well, they seem pretty tense with each other. None of that music and joking around like they do. Haven't had to ask them to quiet down once."

"They shoot ball when they got home?" Gray asked.

"Of course." Doreen had her back to Gray now, working at a bowl of steaming potatoes with a potato masher. "Go wash up, and stick your head in there and tell them boys dinner in five minutes."

"Yes, ma'am."

Gray walked down the hall. Outside Joe's door, he paused a moment, then knocked.

"Yes, 'm?" Joe called out.

Gray opened the door. Joe sat at the little desk they'd bought for him from a second-hand store when he started high school. Shaun stretched out on the floor. They both had notebooks open in front of them, scribbles in purple and green ink.

"Oh, hey Dad," Joe said, stifling a grin. "Thought you were Mom."

"Nope," Gray said. "Shaun, how's your folks?" Shaun's mom and dad ran an office supply store downtown. Good, hard-working folks, Gray thought.

"They're doing good, Mr. Alsobrook, real good."

"Glad to hear it. Supper will be ready in a couple minutes, boys. Y'all come on up to the table."

"Yessir," Joe said.

Gray paused a moment again. He never quite knew what to do around his kids' friends. He wouldn't mind it if they thought he was a nice guy, friendly or funny, but he didn't want to embarrass his kids, either. He ducked back out of Joe's room without saying anything else. Maybe it was best just to be a piece of furniture.

Back at the dining room table, Gray pushed meatloaf and mashed potatoes around his plate, glancing at Doreen between furtive glances up at Joe and Shaun. Shaun used to be a constant fixture at their house after school at least a couple days a week, since he and Joe had met in homeroom the first day of middle school. They'd been in band together, and most classes. Shooting baskets, practicing their music, studying with books and sandwiches piled on the kitchen counter, or laughing and listening to Joe's stereo back in his room, too loud usually, and sometimes staying for supper, particularly the last couple years with the boys old enough to drive themselves to each other's houses. But then something had happened in the fall, involving that black girl Joe had been seeing. Gray pinned it to some jealousy between the boys, but Joe never talked about it and Gray never asked. Shaun had just stopped showing up.

Shaun and Joe were eating quickly. The only noise they made was the working of their jaws as they chewed the meatloaf, and the clank of their forks as they scooped up mashed potatoes.

"What's the project y'all are working on?" Gray asked, about halfway through. Gray wondered if Shaun was part of the protests. He'd always been a happy-seeming kid, and anger and seriousness didn't match up with Gray's thoughts of him.

"Just a school thing we've got due tomorrow," Joe said between mouthfuls.

Shaun nodded and took a large gulp from his glass of milk. "This is good meatloaf, Mrs. Alsobrook," he said after he'd put the glass back down.

"Thanks, Shaun." She glanced at Gray.

Gray cleared his voice. "So, Shaun, what class is y'all's project in?"

Shaun looked at Joe, but Joe seemed particularly focused on his plate as he loaded up his fork for the next bite. "Civics, I guess, sir," Shaun said.

"You 'guess.'"

"Yes, sir. I mean, yes. Civics."

Joe pushed back from the table. "Thanks for dinner, Mom," he said. He stood. "Can we be excused so we can finish up our work?"

Doreen motioned at his plate. "You aren't going to finish?"

"It was good, Mom, but we should really get back to it. I'll eat more later."

"OK. Just put it on the counter. I'll cover it up for you."

Joe and Shaun cleared their plates from the table and walked back down the hallway. Gray listened to the shuffling thuds of their teen-age footsteps until they disappeared behind the soft boom of Joe's door closing, then he looked up at Doreen. She was watching him.

"What about you?" she asked. "You not hungry either? You've been pushing that food all around but barely taken a bite."

"I guess not," Gray said.

"You still thinking about what those folks said on Sunday?"

"I am, I guess. But I honestly don't know whether I'm worried about anything. I don't know if I even should be." The wind gusted harder. The panes of the dining room window rattled loosely in their frames, and Gray heard a crack in the trees outside. There was the sound of metal scraping against concrete on the side porch outside the dining room windows.

"I better go make sure nothing needs to be tied down out there," Gray said, getting up from the table.

He stepped into the kitchen and grabbed his coat off the back of the stool. He shrugged it on as he opened the kitchen door onto the side patio. The cold immediately bit into his cheeks and stung his nose. It was hard to believe that the temperatures were supposed to be like spring behind the coming front, but after twenty years of Alabama weather Gray knew anything was possible at just about any time. If you don't like the weather, wait five minutes, folks always said.

Gray spied the source of the scraping sound. His old wheelbarrow had been turned on its side to not catch water, and the wind had blown it over and pushed it up against the chain-link fence that overlooked the bottomland. He grabbed it by its splintery handles and righted it again, and pulled it over closer to the house, parking it snug up against a lean-to he'd built that he kept tools in. He saw a stack of old paint cans that were probably the next to go, and gathered them up and placed them inside the wheelbarrow. Then he opened up the door to the lean-to and fished out a length of rope. He closed the lean-to door, tied one end of the rope around the door handle, weaved it through the handles of the paint cans, then under the wheelbarrow and back up to the lean-to door, where he tied the other end tight.

"There," he said, the word puffing out in front of him into the cold. Maybe the whole stack would stay put for the night.

Again Gray heard a cracking sound come from the tree-tops. He looked up into the trees that towered over his house. The leaves whipped wildly in the wind. Clouds passed across the moon, covering and uncovering it in quick succession. In the mottled silver light, large limbs stressed at their junctures with the tree trunks. He heard the crack again, and feared one of those limbs might let loose, and who knew where it might go.

But Gray also knew there was nothing he could do for it. He couldn't move the house to somewhere safer. He couldn't tie a rope around every tree limb and lash it to its trunk. The wind would take the limb when it was ready and throw the limb where it wanted.

The kitchen door opened behind Gray. He figured it was Doreen wondering what was taking him so long, so he was surprised when he turned around and Shaun was standing there. He had his backpack slung over one shoulder.

Gray held his hand out to Shaun. "Good seeing you around again, son."

Shaun grabbed Gray's hand and shook it. It was a strong grip. "Yes, sir. Thanks for supper." Shaun went to walk around the side of the house to his car, but stopped after a couple steps and turned. "Mr. Alsobrook?"

"Yes?"

"It's not for civics class, the project."

"I thought it might not be," Gray said.

"I didn't want to lie to you."

Shaun looked at Gray. Gray waited. Shaun looked like he wanted to say something else. But then he just dropped his eyes.

"I'm not upset," Gray said. "I know sometimes y'all got stuff going on."

"Yes, sir," Shaun said, looking back up.

"OK, then." Gray took a step back toward the kitchen door. "Go on home. Tell your folks we said hello."

"I will. Thanks," and Shaun turned and jogged to his car.

Gray went back into the kitchen. The walls and the ceiling felt close. It was a little house, but he felt safe inside it, away from the cold and the wind and whatever else the weather was bringing. It had been a safe place for him and Doreen to raise the girls, and they almost had Joe launched out into the world from it.

Joe leaned against the counter next to the sink, holding his plate and finishing his supper. Doreen was talking to him.

"… but you have to promise me y'all will be careful," she was saying.

Joe looked exasperated, that look he had most times they tried to talk to him, but it was a look that Gray remembered from the girls, too, when they were that age. For a moment, Joe was just Gray's teenaged son, no drama, something Gray could accept and reconcile.

"Of course, Mom," Joe said. "Nobody's going to do anything serious. They all talk a big game, but that's all it is," he said.

Gray put his coat back on the kitchen stool.

"Your Mom's right," he said. "Plenty of cowards in this world. But you haven't been around long enough—hell, we haven't been in this town long enough, none of us, not after twenty years, even—to know when you're crossing over someone's line."

Joe scraped his fork across the plate to get at the last of the mashed potatoes, and didn't look up when he said, "Y'all think I should stop?"

Gray glanced quick at Doreen, then back at Joe. "You've got to think about what you want your relationship to be with this town. But you shouldn't stop if you think this is right."

"Well it is." Joe put his plate into the sink, then looked at Gray. Gray felt like he was looking into a mirror at his own eyes.

GRAY AND DOREEN were driving through Meadowview, Alabama on a rainy day in 1971 when Doreen broke the news.

"You're what?" Gray said to Doreen, incredulous.

"Pregnant," she said. The rain fell down around their car in almost a solid wall, allowing only occasional glimpses of the depressed old downtown along the main drag leading up to the bridge. To Gray, though, it was a bright and sunny day, and this was the best little town in the universe. Gray had just gotten a solid offer on what might be a decent job, so the months-long dry spell since he'd left the service was about to be over. And now this. He slowed the big Ford Galaxy and angled into a parking spot in front of an old storefront. A pink-tubed neon sign hanging from the façade above the green metal awning announced "Carter Drug Co. RX."

"Wow," Gray said. Then he repeated, louder,

his eyes big, "Wow!" He slid across the front bench seat and wrapped Doreen in his arms. Through the windshield and the large window of the pharmacy he saw a skin-and-bones old man with wisps of white hair, watching them. Gray let go of Doreen and pushed back so he could look at her. Her cheeks were flushed, a smile beginning to strain her cheeks, but he thought he saw some worry in her eyes.

"So we'll have three of them back there," Doreen said, cocking her head in the direction of the back seat.

"I guess so." Gray ran the fingers of his right hand through his hair. It was finally starting to bush out from the military buzz he'd worn it in for nine years. Then he felt a flash of the anxiety that had come upon him from time to time in the past few months.

"Hey," Doreen said, putting a hand on his arm, "I see that look. Don't you start worrying about any of this. It's all coming together. You're doing good!" Seeing her smile, feeling the steadiness and smooth warmth of her palm on his forearm, Gray knew she was right.

He looked back at her and grinned. "So I guess I ought to take that job then." Gray laughed. He was probably going to take it anyway. They'd been staying long enough with Doreen's parents in Little Rock, where the girls were while he and Doreen drove down to Alabama for Gray to interview at the paper mill looking for a shop foreman. Not the most glamorous job or glamorous place in the world, but it came with the promise of advancement and settling down. More than anything, Gray was ready for that, for settling down. After the years of moving around from base to base, and after he'd decided not to re-up a few months back, he'd heard about what had happened to Big Joe at the final end of all his wandering.

"So is this the place, then?" Doreen asked, looking out the car windows. A tall black man in a tan suit and a brown tie, a brown fedora on his head, and a battered black umbrella in his hand to shelter him from the rain, walked briskly along the sidewalk, looking at them out of the side of his eye as he passed the front of their car. No one else was on the street. "Meadowview?"

"That's what they said at the mill, that most folks either live here or in Thomasville, but the schools are better here." Gray and Doreen looked out the windows. "The big city," Gray said, a wry smile on his face. The rain was slacking off some, but was still coming down. The downtown stretched in either direction up and down the street. They could see the bridge over the Alabama River a couple blocks in one direction, and the bell towers of a cluster of downtown churches in the other.

"I guess it can't be any worse off than being in Little Rock," Doreen said, "and close enough that my folks can still come visit."

"Hmph," Gray said. He would be glad for some space, he thought, space he could lay claim to. "You know," he said, "if it's a boy..." He looked over at Doreen's stomach, just barely rounded, what he had previously thought maybe was just eating her mom's home-cooking for the past half a year and not the result of anything they'd done after he returned from that last tour.

"Yes?"

"I want to name him Joe." The thought was clear to him only the moment he said it, and it felt right.

"Are you sure? I thought you didn't want

anything to do with that name?"

"You know, Big Joe's dead now. He doesn't get to take that to the grave with him." He wanted to add *the sorry son of a bitch*, but out of respect for the dead he left it unsaid. A couple weeks after he and Doreen and the girls had showed up in Little Rock, an attorney had called him, told him Big Joe had been dead of a heart attack seven months before. There'd been a will that mentioned Gray. There'd been no kind of inheritance, but the probate attorney had kept a note to try to track Gray down if he could.

"So what would it be, then," Doreen asked, her voice sounding gentle in Gray's ears, "Joseph Gray Alsobrook the fourth?"

Gray thought about it for a moment. The rain slacked the rest of the way off. He cranked down the car window and fingered a cigarette from the pack in his shirt pocket. "Naw," he said. "He'll be his own man. And we ain't royalty, anyways. Why don't we give him your daddy's name, too?"

"Joseph Alan Alsobrook," Doreen said. "I like that."

Gray lit the cigarette, then pulled the Galaxy back out into the street, headed for Little Rock to pick up the girls.

ON WEDNESDAY, Gray left the noise of the mill's shop behind in the early afternoon, telling Cyrus that he had an appointment to see about his knee.

"All right, boss," Cyrus said, waving him out.

The hour's drive back to town over crawling-log-truck two-lane roads seemed less numbing than it usually was at the end of a day. Gray tapped his knee with one hand while he worked the steering wheel, passing trucks and beat-up old cars whenever there was a straightaway. He was less worried whether he'd miss the march than whether the marchers would miss the storm. Clouds were already pouring in from the west, ahead of the threatened front. It wasn't supposed to start coming down until in the night, but the sky looked sinister. Part of Gray hoped they'd call off the march. He pressed down a little more urgently on the gas pedal.

When Gray told Doreen Wednesday morning he planned to leave work early, she'd asked, incredulous, "Gray Alsobrook going to a march?"

"I ain't going to be *in* the march, Doreen. I just want to make sure Joe's all right."

"You know you can't pull him out of it, right?" Doreen had asked.

"He won't even know I'm there."

Gray slowed when he entered town. It was just a quarter after three, so there was no need to rush. The streets were still dry. Ten minutes later, he pulled into a parking spot about a block from the Board of Education building. With the high school probably a twenty-minute march away and school having just let out, he had time to have a smoke and check out the surroundings. He cranked his window down. The wind, still bitter despite the warm air coming, blew in even fiercer gusts than the night before.

A small group of news reporters and photographers stood by the front steps of the education building, gathered in a knot with their jacket collars turned up, probably talking scuttlebutt while they waited for the kids to arrive. He knew there'd be the *Times-Journal's* folks, for sure. Probably someone from the *Advertiser* over in Montgomery. Maybe even as far away as Birmingham. He'd heard there'd even been some fellow down from Cincinnati asking questions over the weekend. Wouldn't be long before reporters from the networks showed up. Folks ate up a juicy race story.

Between the education building and where he was, a dark blue American sedan was parked in another spot, with three men inside. They were all dressed in suit coats and ties and sunglasses. One of them was fiddling with a bulky video camera. They all looked like they were laughing, turning to each other every now and then but mainly looking in the other direction, toward where the marchers would be coming from the school. Gray figured he'd make sure they stayed between him and the education building, so he could keep an eye on them.

Gray lit a second cigarette and got out to lean against the side of his truck. The darkened sky took on an almost greenish hue. Skies like that promised nothing good.

The first sign the marchers were nearing was the unknotting of the gaggle of reporters by the school building, as they turned their attention down the street. The photographers got their cameras ready, lens caps tucked in jacket pockets, gloves off and fingers ready to work. Then the suited men in the sedan came to attention in their car, eyes and video camera trained down the road. Then Gray heard faint snatches of chants on the gusts of wind.

As the students came into view in the next block, Gray saw they were all dressed in black. In front of the larger mass of kids, six students carried a coffin, and behind them two more held a banner. "Bury Injustice," Gray made out from the writing on the banner as they neared the steps of the education building. Then, behind the banner-bearers, Gray saw Joe, the one white face among forty or fifty black marchers, chanting in unison, arms locked. And as they got closer, the snippets of chant became a song in Gray's ears. "We shall overcome," they sang, until they were arrayed in front of the education building.

The handful at the front of the larger group, Joe among them, mounted the steps of the building, and the two banner bearers slid in behind them, raising the banner high. The pall-bearers set their coffin down at the foot of the steps. Gray wondered if all the news cameras were aimed at Joe. He wondered what Blaine and Jimbo and the rest would have to say at the coffee table on Sunday. Surely they'd all see his son now, not smeared in blood, proud, lifting a deer's head by the antlers at the back of the sports section, but front page, black and white, a protest song on his lips.

Each of the student leaders up on the steps took turns speaking. Gray could only catch the occasional word, not enough to put them together. He wished one of them had thought to bring a megaphone. At least the students could hear themselves, as they would murmur or clap or occasionally cheer in breaks in the speeches.

After three of the black student leaders had spoken, Joe stepped to the center of the steps. Now Gray really wished that the kids had thought of some way to amplify their voices. He didn't want his first hearing of what Joe said to be when he read it in the paper the next morning. The cheering of the gathered marchers seemed like it might be louder in the breaks in whatever Joe was saying. Gray felt a mixture of pride and anxiety for Joe.

Gray began to slide out from where he stood behind his truck, thinking maybe he could get a better vantage by walking up behind the sedan with the men in it.

But as Gray went to step on the sidewalk, a handful of large boys, white kids, polo shirts stretching across football player torsos and tucked into faded jeans, loafers and tennis shoes, brushed by him, walking toward the education building. They kept walking until they were just past the sedan. One of the men in the car turned his head toward them, then back to where Joe was still speaking on the steps.

The group of white boys lined out. Slightly in front of the rest, Gray recognized Baxter Cranston, Blaine's step-son. Blaine complained about Baxter every few weeks, his young second wife's son. A mailbox-basher and weekend pot-smoker. Blaine had kept him out of trouble with the police so far.

At the next pause in Joe's speech, between the cheer and the next sentence, Baxter yelled out, "Race-traitor!" His gang of preppy rednecks yelled out, "Yeah!" behind him, as if to back him up, though to Gray they looked nervous, ready to bolt. But Joe kept on talking. Only a few students in the back of the crowd turned and looked at the white boys.

Then another of the boys yelled out, "Hey, faggot! Shut your dick-hole!" Baxter turned and poked the yeller in his ribs, but then high-fived him. Now four students in the crowd, two large boys and a couple girls, turned completely around and took a step toward the boys. At the same time, a cheer went up from the rest of the students. Everyone looked up toward the steps again.

At the top of the steps, the door had opened, and the superintendent, Russell Livaudais, stepped out. He held both hands up and out toward the students, but they only cheered harder. The white boys fell quiet. The superintendent walked down the steps to the knot of student leaders, put a hand on

Joe's shoulder and leaned in to say something in his ear, then Joe stood aside for the superintendent.

When the students quieted down, Livaudais's deep voice carried clearly so that even Gray could make it out.

"Thank you," he called out to the students. "Thank you for making an effort, and for speaking out." Cheers, but then a respectful silence.

"These decisions will be made by those who have been chosen to make them, but know that they hear you." Livaudais pointed up to the building behind him. He paused and glanced toward the knot of white boys, his face hardening for a moment before shifting his eyes back to the gathered students.

"You are amazing students," he called out. "All of you. Your determination is admirable. And that your methods are peaceful," he paused, letting that word sink in, "is the best thing to your credit. Do not let that go." The students cheered again, and kept cheering as Livaudais turned and walked back up the steps. He turned and waved one more time before going in the door and closing it behind him.

The knot of white boys turned and walked back toward Gray. They were elbowing each other and saying amongst themselves, "showed them" and "damn niggers" and "fucking faggot," even laughing, as they walked by. Baxter threw a conspiratorial smirk toward Gray as they passed.

Gray turned back toward the education building. The students were gathering back into a looser formation, clumps of them already headed back up the street toward the school. Gray looked, hard among the groups of departing students, but couldn't see Joe.

"Daddy," called out a voice from across the

street, to Gray's right, startling him. Joe must've seen him and walked down the street toward him on the other side.

"Joe, come on," he said. "I'll give you a lift."

Joe looked at the departing students, then back across at Gray. "All right." Before he could step off the sidewalk to cross the street, the sedan with the men in suits backed out of its space, and drove toward them. The sedan drove slowly, and the man in the passenger seat with the video camera aimed his camera first at Joe, then, as they drew adjacent to them, turned and focused in on Gray. They neither slowed nor sped up, but kept driving steadily by and in the direction of City Hall, toward the river.

"That was strange," Joe said as he crossed in the wake of the car.

"Yeah," Gray said as he opened the driver's side door of his truck. "Strange day." He got in and slammed his door.

Joe climbed into the passenger side of the truck. "Strange town," he said.

Gray pulled out and headed toward the school. He looked over at Joe, but Joe was staring out his window. He figured he should say something. "Good thing y'all got it in before the rain."

"Hm," was all Joe said in response. Then he sighed.

"Something wrong?"

Joe looked forward out the windshield. He opened his mouth as if gearing up to say something, closed it, then opened it again, finally saying, quietly, "Just don't know any of this is going to do any good."

WEDNESDAY NIGHT, the storms started. Lightning flashed, showing trees bending from the sky toward the ground, and thunder crashed down so hard that even Joe came out of his bedroom to watch the weather with Gray and Doreen. Again Gray had the illusion that Joe was a young kid still, scared out of his room and into his parents' room by a summer storm, except now it was winter and Joe was bigger and Gray couldn't reconcile this vision with what he'd seen that afternoon at the march.

The radar on the television screen glowed yellow and orange and red. The counties just to their west were covered by tornado warnings, and there was no reason to believe the same wouldn't come through their county later in the night.

After everyone was in bed again, Gray lay and listened for a freight train roar to separate from the general howling of the wind, until he was asleep. He woke to a jarring ring. It was still dark, but the winds had quieted. He heard the ringing again, and shot his hand out to catch the phone receiver from its cradle before it woke the whole house.

"Hello?"

"This Gray Alsobrook?" a man asked on the other end of the line, clearly trying to mask his voice in a low croak.

"What is it?" Gray whispered into the phone.

"Your son better watch himself," said the man.

"Who is this?"

"You all better watch yourselves." And then the line clicked dead.

"Who was that?" Doreen mumbled from her pillow. Gray sighed.

"Just a wrong number," he said.

1978 WAS THE HOTTEST SUMMER since they'd moved to Meadowview. Joe was six years old, and

Gray found himself up at the city pool not far from their house many evenings after he got home from the mill and most weekends. It was always crowded, and Gray would keep an eye on Joe while sneaking sips from a sixer of cold beer he kept in a brown bag by his feet. The evenings were hot, the heat encasing them all in a sheen of sweat, with the air totally still, through the end of May and into June.

Doreen's job was the more difficult one, it seemed to Gray, watching over Lilah and Ruthie, now 15 and 13, as they hung around with a group of teens in a clump of stretched-out towels and deck chairs by the high dive. A group of mothers, mainly, talked and laughed near the teens, pretending not to be watching hawk-like over their kids. Gray would've had a stroke over there, so he was fine with his job watching Joe.

By the shallow end and the adjacent baby pool, the territory where Joe roamed, parents kept more to themselves and the kids weren't up to anything nefarious, not like the middle kids or the teens arrayed through the deep end and by the diving board. The worst thing Gray had to deal with was clueless kids who might wander over and pick up one of Joe's pool toys to play with, not to steal it but just because they figured it was lying around waiting for someone to play with it. Even that was anxiety enough for Gray. He'd watch as Joe puzzled out how to react. Joe never seemed to care, but Gray would then try to keep mental inventory of the various toys as they moved around the pool area, scooping them up as soon as they were abandoned by whatever kid had appropriated them. Those kids' parents ought to teach them better, he figured, or bring their own pool toys.

The summer of 1978 was also the first summer the public pool on the east side of town was closed, and black families were showing up at the main city pool on the west side for the first time. Gray hadn't thought much about it until one sultry evening after work at the beginning of June. Gnats were starting to rise up as the sun sank, but the heat was still hours from breaking for the night. Gray was stretched out on a chair by a table watching Joe and sipping his beer when one of the other white dads sat next to him and announced, "Ain't bringing my girls back here after tonight. Ain't right. Them burrheads pissing and sweating and snotting in the same water as our kids."

Gray looked hard at the man to figure if he should recognize him from church or the mill or something, because he couldn't figure out why the man had just told him this. "Excuse me?" Gray said.

The man continued, "Well, you know they got them weird African viruses."

Gray laughed then and said, "Shoot, I hear you might catch that black, too. What if your girls turn black?"

"Hey, buddy, screw you," the man said, sitting up on the edge of his chair, looking at Gray with a bewildered look on his face. Then he stood up and stomped over to a different table.

Gray didn't see that man any more at the pool. In fact, he noticed several other of the white families disappeared over the next couple weeks, but steadily a few more black families seemed to show up on a regular basis, too, and all in all it was only slightly more crowded than previous summers. By mid-June, Gray was back to his usual worries of keeping track of Joe's things, trying not to worry about how small his girls' swimsuits were over in that hive of boys on the other end.

Most of the kids in the pool seemed to settle

back into their standard patterns, too. Sharks and minnows, races, splashing, dunking, horseplay, diving, Marco Polo, and all the rest.

On the Saturday afternoon before the Fourth of July, Gray was with the family at the pool. As usual, it was hot, and it was crowded with families. Two beers into the afternoon, Gray heard shouting coming from out in the parking lot and noticed some of the other parents had gotten up and walked over to the fence. Joe was in the middle of a holding-breath competition with some black kid about the same size who he'd been playing with the previous few times at the pool, them taking turns going under while the other one counted, so Gray got up from his chair and walked over to the tall chain-link fence that separated the pool from the parking lot to see what was going on.

Seven or eight Klansmen marched back and forth in a picket line between the parked cars and the pool fence, white robes, pointed hoods, but no masks, their faces red and belligerent, shouting, "Protect our children! Coloreds go home! Protect our children! Coloreds go home!" on and off, shouting it a few times, then falling silent in their march, then shouting it four or five more times, a little louder.

One of the black dads standing near Gray said, though not too loud, "You go home," but the Klansmen either didn't hear him or didn't care. Gray looked over his shoulder and saw that many of the parents had started to situate themselves between the fence and the pool, while most of the kids kept playing, not noticing. By the teens near the diving board, one large white boy turned up a boom box that had been playing a local radio station, as loud as it would go. A couple of white families with smaller children gathered up their things and their kids, and some of them quickly left out the gate and edged around the marching Klansmen to their cars.

Gray felt a hand on his arm and looked beside him. Doreen was there.

"Honey, we should take the kids home," she said.

"This can't be serious," Gray answered. "You can't just let these assholes scare us off."

"I'm not scared, Gray Alsobrook," Doreen said, "and you know it. I don't want our kids to have to see this. It's ugly."

Most of the other men who had walked over to the fence had gone back to the pool, closer to their kids, closer to their wives. Probably trying to figure out what to do, too, just like Doreen and him. The dad who had quietly told the Klansmen to go home still stood at the fence, arms crossed over his chest, his face looking like it was on the verge of twisting into a scowl or a shout. The Klansmen let out another chorus of "Protect our children! Coloreds go home!"

"Just go back over by the pool and keep an eye on the kids for a bit," Gray said.

"What are you going to do?" Doreen wrapped both hands around his arm, pressing him, like the heat.

"I'm just going to go talk to them," he said. "Now go where you can watch the kids. Please." Gray saw a police car at the back of the lot, parked close to the street, the cop inside with his window rolled down, watching the Klansmen, an unconcerned look on his face.

"Be careful," Doreen said, and turned and walked over to the edge of the pool where Joe was laughing at something his new friend had said.

Gray walked to the gate, keeping an eye on the Klansmen. One of them, a tall, lanky fellow in little round-lensed glasses, watched him while the rest let out another round of shouting. "Protect our children! Coloreds go home!" Gray opened the gate and crossed the small strip of grass and sidewalk to the picket line. The one who'd been watching him stepped out of the procession.

"What you want?" he challenged Gray, with a smile on his lips that didn't extend to the rest of his face.

"Why don't y'all just go on," Gray said. "You made your point."

"Fella, we ain't leaving 'til them coloreds are gone from here or they close the place." He was taller than Gray by a good five or six inches, and his white robe only fell about to his knees, paint-spattered khaki work pants and boots underneath. He looked down into Gray's face without blinking.

Gray looked over his shoulder toward the pool. The black dad who'd retorted earlier was still at the fenceline, and a handful of white and black dads had separated from the parents by the pool and were arrayed slightly behind him. They weren't necessarily trying to show any force. There was clearly some indecision about what their role would be, between the laughing kids, the worried wives, and Gray and the other dad who were confronting the marching Klan. Gray knew it was a tough spot for everyone, and he wasn't quite sure why he'd put himself in the front of it. Gray looked back at the tall hooded man in front of him.

"There's children here. Please," Gray said, "y'all go on home now."

"It's our children we aim to protect," the

Klansman said, almost yelling. "We don't want them getting mixed up with each other. It ain't right. It ain't what's intended."

"Take your children across the street, then," Gray said, getting louder, too, and pointed beyond the Klansman toward the town's Country Club, surrounded by pristine golf greens, its white clubhouse haunched on thick columns, serene, just across the street from the municipal recreation complex.

The Klansman let out a snort, then laughed, his amusement stretching up to his eyes. "Fella, you something else. I ain't got that kind of money, and they probably wouldn't have me anyway." He stopped laughing. "Why don't you just take your nigger friends and make your own damn club."

"Look, mister," Gray said, trying to sound firm, "if y'all don't choose to go home on your own, then I'll get that police officer over there to make y'all go." Gray tried to stand up as tall as he could, but the Klansman laughed again.

"That's something, buddy. That cop's with us."

Before Gray could think what to say next, from behind him he heard a shout, loud, repeated, insistent, in a solitary voice: "Go. Home. Go. Home. Go. Home." He looked behind him. It was the dad who had retorted earlier, shouting, one word at a time, pumping his fist into the air with each word. Three other black men separated from the grouped parents and took a step toward the fence, each joining in the new chant. "Go. Home. Go. Home. Go. Home." Their fists, too, slowly went into the air and joined the first man's. The white parents just watched and looked unsure.

At that moment, the sound of a police siren startled Gray to turn back around. The one cop car from the back of the lot screeched into motion and sped toward the pool. At the same time, two more police cars came speeding from a side street where they had been out of view. All three cars squealed to a stop between the Klansmen and the pool fence.

"All right, all of you," crackled a voice through a speaker atop one of the police cars. "This pool is closed." Three cops got out of one of the new cars to join the one from the car that had been in the lot, and four got out of another. Only one stayed behind in a car to continue his directions over the speaker.

"What do you mean, closed?" called out one of the dads at the fence.

"We ain't done nothing here, officer," yelled another one. "It's those Kluxers causing all the trouble."

"Now that's it," crackled the cop through the speaker, "No more of that riot language. Clear the pool in five minutes and no one gets arrested."

The men inside the fence looked at the cops in disbelief, then at each other, then back at the families by the pool. Everyone was watching, the kids' yells and laughter quieted. One of them said, "We'll take it to the City Council." Someone else said, "or the court," and the officer on the speaker crackled, "Five minutes. Once the pool's closed, y'all will be trespassing."

The Klansmen stood in a line watching the police and the activity inside the pool fence. Children swam to the edges of the pool to pull themselves out, mothers corralled kids into towels to dry off, and dads began stuffing belongings into bags, shaking their heads. Gray saw Doreen and the kids come out of the gate.

"Come on, Gray," Doreen called out to him as she herded the kids toward the side street for the walk home.

Gray jogged over to his family, and grabbed up Joe's hand in his. Joe kept looking over his shoulder at the scene in the parking lot. Car doors were slamming, other families were still filtering out the gate, young kids screaming and unhappy.

"Who are those men, Daddy?" Joe asked Gray.

"Ignorant fools," Gray said.

"Are they why we had to leave?"

"They'll be gone tomorrow," Gray said. "We'll come back then. We live here, Joe. Don't ever forget that. They can't chase us off. You hear?"

"Yessir," and Joe turned back to their walk.

But they couldn't get back in the next day, or any day through the Fourth of July weekend, either. A padlock was closed tight on the gate, with signs that read, "Pool closed." By the middle of July, the pool was drained and dump trucks full of dirt showed up. A section of fence was removed and they dumped their loads into the pool, one load after another, for two weeks. Men, black men mostly, with shovels, were dropped off at the end of each day to move the dirt around and even it up, and at the end of two weeks the dirt was an even fill, a foot below the lip of the pool all the way around. At the beginning of August, the cement trucks showed up. In three days, a concrete cap had leveled off the rest of the pool. By the middle of August, the fence was rebuilt all the way around, and that was the end of the summer of 1978.

THURSDAY WASN'T as bad as Gray feared it would be. Tornadoes had touched down nearby in the night, but in sparsely populated farmland just outside the town's fringes, like a reminder or a threat. In town, there were downed tree limbs, some shingles blown off roofs here and there, a lot of bleary eyes from storm-interrupted sleep, but no one hurt, nothing destroyed.

And the front page of the paper was devoted to the odd weather, a picture of a gas station canopy toppled over in Mississippi from the afternoon before. There was a picture of Joe at the march, slightly blurry and off-center in the frame, the photo focused instead on the superintendent on the steps, but folks had to open the paper to page three to see even that.

The promised heat had definitely blown in behind the storms. Mid-January, and the temperature reached 79 in the afternoon, where the day before the high had been 50. Gray was sweating in the shop. All the men were.

Friday was even warmer because the nighttime temps hadn't gone too far down into the 60s. By eleven in the morning, Cyrus asked Gray if they could open the shop bay door, the big overhead door they raised up to drive in the large skidders and tractor-trucks. A warm breeze, like spring, swept in the large opening, and Gray's crew smiled as they continued their work.

At noon, the mill's break whistle blew. Gray finished checking through a cabinet of cables and belts, marking off a checklist to figure out the next week's parts order, then he joined Cyrus, Willie, and Tom at the little table and chairs outside his office door. Tom and Cyrus were halfway through cold-cut sandwiches. Willie was spooning large chunks of meat from a thermos, a scowl on his face.

"Soup, Willie?" Gray asked. He pulled his own sandwich from a crumpled brown bag, then pulled an apple out and set it down next to it.

"Beef stew. Cel made it Sunday," Willie said. "It was still cold on Sunday. Stew was good then."

The men laughed. Gray liked not worrying

about anything momentous, even for just a short time. The phone started ringing in his office.

"Damnit," he said as he got up from the table without having taken a bite of his sandwich.

"Yo," he said into the phone. "Shop. Alsobrook."

Doreen was on the other end. "Have you heard?" she asked.

"What are you talking about, honey?"

"They're sending kids home from the schools. I don't know what's going on. My shift's not over until five. Someone said something about a riot at the high school, and someone else said it was at the junior high, then someone else said it's nothing but rumors."

"Slow down, Doreen," Gray said. "Now if the schools are shutting early, Joe's got his car and he'll come on home. And if they aren't, he'll be fine."

"How can you say that, Gray?" Gray heard the panic in her voice, and he started to get concerned. Doreen was always the solid one in the family, the one who could make all the plans and make sure everything got done.

"You should've seen him Wednesday afternoon," Gray said. "There's a lot of kids at that school who like him and believe in him. He won't be in any trouble." But Gray also thought about the small group of white boys and their taunts, and he wondered who exactly was causing what kind of trouble.

"All right," she said. "You're probably right. If I hear anything more, I'll call you back?"

"You know you can call me here whenever you want, babe."

There was a pause on the other end, then, "I love you, Gray."

"I love you, too, Doreen." Gray peeked out his office door. The other men were talking low to each other at the table while they kept eating. "I won't be late tonight," he added before hanging up.

Gray went back out and ate his sandwich quickly, put his apple back in the sack.

"You ain't hungry, boss?" Tom said.

"Naw," Gray answered. "Would rather get some of this nice day out there before the whistle blows again."

"Heard that," Tom said.

Gray walked over to the bay door and stepped outside. The constant din of the mill's machinery filled the day as it always did, the screaming of saws, the knocks of various pipes and hammers, the grinding of gears, and behind it all the low, constant roar of the fires in the boiler, generating the power to run it all.

Gray pulled his pack of smokes out of his shirt pocket and fished out a cigarette. He thought about Joe at the march the day before, and about the kids clapping for him. He thought about the white boys and their insults. He thought about the black kids who had started to break from the larger group to confront the white boys. "Damnit," he said again, softly in an exhaled cloud of cigarette smoke. He threw his cigarette down to the ground, half-smoked, and smashed it into the dirt with his steel-toed boot.

"Cyrus," he called out as he stalked back into the shop. "I've got to go."

"You all right?" Cyrus asked.

"I'm fine, but there's something going on in town. I have to go check on Joe." Gray was already into his office, looking for his keys.

"He all right?" Cyrus leaned against the frame of Gray's office door.

"I'm sure he is." Gray stopped to look around his desk, make sure there wasn't some invoice or bit of paperwork that needed his immediate attention. Then he looked back up at Cyrus. He could see the genuine concern on the man's face. It struck him that, if he weren't the boss, in some other world they could be friends. "I hope he is," he said. "I just have to go see about him."

Gray drove fast, flashing through the countryside, but the hour to town never seemed longer. He kept thinking about the look Baxter Cranston had thrown him as the pack of boys had left down the sidewalk on Wednesday. *Damn niggers* echoed in his head. *Fucking faggot. Watch yourself.*

Gray's drive into town brought him past his house, Joe's car not in the driveway, so he kept driving straight on to the high school, sitting on Broad Street in the middle of town. He turned into the long driveway that went up into a horseshoe at the front doors. The parking lots to either side of the drive were empty, and a lone police cruiser was parked at the apex of the horseshoe. Gray pulled his company truck in behind the cruiser and put it in park, not even stopping to turn the engine off or take the keys from the ignition before he swung the door open and got out to walk over to the driver's door of the cop car.

A large white cop sat in the driver's seat, semi-reclined, the window open. He looked up at Gray through mirrored lenses.

"School's closed, mister. Can I help you?"

Gray looked from the cop up to the school's front doors. A chain hung loosely from one of the door handles, no lock attaching its ends, and the door was slightly cracked open.

"I'm looking for my son. He ain't at home," Gray said, "and I thought... Well, sometimes he's involved with things at the school."

"Forty kids in the cafeteria," the cop said, "having a sit-in or some foolishness, but your son ain't in there."

Gray didn't know this cop, not that he knew of. "Can I go in and be sure?"

The cop looked at Gray for a moment, his jowls hanging loosely, then he said, "Hang on." He pulled the handset from his radio and toggled it. "Yo Billy, there any white kids in there?"

Gray heard a voice come back over the radio speaker. "Naw, just black ones."

The cop in the car looked up at Gray, his eyebrows raised over the tops of his sunglasses. "You check with his friends?" he asked.

Gray hadn't. "No. I just thought he might be here. Thanks for the help." Gray turned to walk back to his truck.

The cop called out, "You be sure to let us know if you don't track him down," but Gray was already in his driver's seat and putting the truck in gear.

As he drove back up the long drive toward the street, he saw two more cop cars go speeding back toward downtown, followed a moment later by a van from one of the Montgomery TV stations. Gray turned in the same direction and followed as close as he dared. After rumbling over the L&N crossing and taking a couple turns, Gray figured they were headed for the Board of Education building.

Again, Gray parked a block away, but this time it was because he had to, no parking spots any closer. A small crowd was gathered outside the building, where the two cop cars had pulled up. Gray got out of his truck and walked quickly up the street toward the building. As he approached, the police officers opened the back door of one of the cruisers and escorted two well-dressed, older white men, school board members, through a crowd of parents packed on the steps and going into the building. The crowd seemed evenly mixed, black and white, and Gray recognized the parents of some of the kids from Joe's class in among them. Gray heard shouts of "What are you going to do?" and "Fire him!" and "Sign his contract!" The school board members disappeared behind the police into the front doors of the building.

The crowd began to file up the stairs and squeeze in the door behind them. Gray asked an older black woman walking up the steps next to him, "What's happening?"

"Emergency school board meeting," she said. "They going to do something about what happened over at the junior high."

"What happened at the junior high?"

The lady looked at Gray. "Nobody really knows, but they all say they do. None of them were there, but they're saying kids got pushed down in the halls. Trying to set us up and blame somebody." She kept walking up the stairs. Gray followed.

He squeezed down the hall and through the door of the school board's meeting room, the last person to make it through. The room was packed. All the benches were filled shoulder-to-shoulder, and along the walls parents stood, squeezed in next to each other. So many were talking that they were shouting to be heard over each other. At the front of the room, the eleven board members—six white and five black—were seated at a long table, with a florid-faced man with a shock of white hair in the center, the school board president, banging a gavel on the table-top. In front of them, at a small table between the board members and the chaotic audience, sat Dr.

Livaudais, facing the board members, waiting.

"Everyone please quiet down," the board president shouted, "Please. So we can get started. It's been a long day for everyone." Slowly, the crowd quieted down to a murmur and a scattering of cleared throats and grumbles. "Now, Dr. Livaudais, thank you for accommodating us. It's come to some of our attention that your continued presence is creating a distraction, and some would say a dangerous situation, for the students."

"This isn't right," one of the black school board members, an older man down at the end of the table, said.

"Now, Hiram," the board president said, "just hold on. Please. We'll all get a vote on what to do. But first I want to know what Dr. Livaudais has to say about all this." They all turned and looked at the superintendent.

"Well," he said, "I'm here to do a job. I think I've been doing a good job for three years. I only think the students are trying to tell us that they agree. Nobody asked them in the review. That being said, I serve at the will of this Board, and I respect the process. Now I've had reports back from the principals at the schools today. The calls we've had from some parents had alarmed us that there had been some event at the junior high, but that turns out to have been misreported. There were a handful of kids outside one of the classrooms when that classroom was letting out. Some of them weren't entirely watching out where they were going, and perhaps were being inconsiderate of others, and two students fell down in the hall. None were hurt. We have some students who will be called in to speak to the principal in the morning about what happened. This is no different than discipline issues that happen everyday, and there's no reason to think it's related to any of the lawful protests that other students have been engaged in."

The murmuring in the crowd grew louder when Dr. Livaudais was finished, and the school board president gaveled the room back into silence.

Hiram Weeks, the older black school board member who had spoken up before, said to the school board president, "I'm satisfied, Dr. Morgan, and I don't think any action is necessary. I think calling this emergency meeting was ill-advised."

"Our parents in this district were concerned, Hiram," the president returned, "and we must be responsible to them. Any motions?"

One of the white woman school board members, to the other side of the president, raised her hand. "I move that we amend the contract status of Dr. Russell Livaudais, and terminate him from his position immediately." The room broke out in loud shouts.

"You can't do that!" yelled out one woman from the middle of the room. Dr. Livaudais sat silently at his table. The school board president banged his gavel.

"I will have the police clear this room if the audience will not quiet down!" he called out over the din. "This will be an orderly public meeting, or the public will be asked to leave." He continued to bang his gavel. Three uniformed officers stood out from the crowd and filed in behind the table of board members, and the crowd again quieted.

A spectacled, short white board member at the end of the table raised his hand. "I second Edie's motion," he said.

"All in favor of the motion to terminate Dr. Russell Livaudais's contract immediately," said the board president, "say aye."

"AYE," spoke out all six white board members, in unison.

"All opposed?" the president asked, and turned to look down the side of the table where the five black school board members sat.

Hiram pushed his chair back form the table and stood. "I will not participate in this vote," he said. "It is illegal, and reprehensible." He then pushed past the crowd, brushing past Gray on his way to and then out the door. The other four black school board members also stood, and filed out of the room.

"The remaining board members are a quorum," the president announced, "and have voted, six to nothing, and the motion carries. Dr. Livaudais, thank you for your service. This meeting is adjourned."

Gray slipped out the door as the room erupted once more.

Gray drove back home. Joe's car was in the driveway. When Gray got out of his truck, he heard the hollow bounce of the basketball against the concrete pad in the backyard, the rattle of the ball on the metal rim of the goal. He walked around the side of the house and found Joe alone, shooting baskets with a small purple shiner sitting above his right eye.

"You all right, son?"

Joe stopped dribbling and held the basketball loosely between his hand and his hip. He'd worked up a sweat. "It's nothing, Dad. I've got this."

Gray held his hands out for the ball. Joe bounce-passed it to him, one pneumatic thunk against the concrete between them. "Your mother's not going to like the looks of that." Gray held the ball up above his head, eyed the rim of the basket twenty feet away, pumped his arms back and lofted the ball toward the goal. It banged high off the backboard and bounced toward Joe.

"I can't help that," Joe said, dribbling the ball back up into his hands. He hooked it in an arc high over his head. It dropped through the bottom of the net.

As Joe slow-walked over to grab the ball, Gray hustled up to him and boxed him out with his hip, scooped the ball up himself.

"Dad!" Joe said.

Gray held onto the ball with both hands. "Son, you promised to be careful, and I trust you to be going about this right. Were you over at the junior high today?"

Joe looked at Gray for a second. "No. I don't even know what went on over there."

"Well, what happened then?" Gray asked, looking at the darkened patch covering Joe's eyebrow. "Don't tell me it was nothing. Too much has been going on in this town today for it to be nothing."

"Give me the ball, Dad. Come on," Joe said, holding his hands out.

"Did one of the other protesting kids do that to you?"

"No, Dad. It wasn't that." He dropped his arms back to his side.

"Was it that Baxter Cranston, or one of his friends, then?"

Joe said nothing.

"It was, wasn't it. I'll go drive over to his dad's office right now."

"No, Dad. Leave it be. I started it." Joe stepped toward Gray and put his hands on the ball. Gray held it tighter.

"You're just saying what you think is right, Joe. You didn't start a fight."

"No, today, they were yelling shit at my friends, so I ran and tackled one of them. It was me, Dad. I started it. I don't even know if it was one of them or the parking lot that did this to my face. Just drop it."

Gray stepped back from Joe and let the ball drop between them. "Put some ice on it, Joe. I'll talk to your mom when she gets home."

ON THE FOLLOWING MONDAY, Gray and Doreen sat in the anteroom outside the superintendent's office in mismatched, cracked-leather chairs, Joe in between them. Gray should've been at work. The main fire engine from the mill's emergency department was in the shop, the cab tilted backwards and all Gray's guys working on the engine. Instead, Gray was back in town, waiting to find out what would happen to Joe, after a call from Doreen that they were both to go with him.

Vice-principals at the high school—white assistant football coaches with too much damned power, thought Gray—wanted to expel him. Said they had multiple witnesses that Joe was swigging alcohol from a jar before he tackled the Cranston kid's friend, and that the other kid got the worst of it. That was all Doreen knew when she called him and told him to meet her at the Board of Education building.

The superintendent's office door had been closed since they got there and the secretary told them to have a seat. Gray wondered who would be at the desk since the previous week's firing. He wondered if there was some vice-superintendent or line of succession. Probably some mayor's stooge. He really needed to be back at the shop.

The office door opened up, and the white board president backed slowly out, a smile on his face. "Well, glad you're back, Russell, glad you're back."

Dr. Livaudais followed him out, and clapped him on the shoulder. "We have unfinished business, Carl. Let's get this done." He looked down at the Alsobrooks, then back at the board president. "Let me get back to work."

The board president looked down at Joe, sitting between Gray and Doreen, and his smile flattened into a thin line. "Yes, I see you need to do that."

"Joe, Mr. and Mrs. Alsobrook," Dr. Livaudais said, "come on in my office. This won't take long." Joe was the first one up out of his chair and following him into his office, ahead of his parents.

"But, Doc, I thought you were fired," Joe said, standing by Dr. Livaudais's desk while the superintendent walked around to the other side to sit down in his big desk chair.

Dr. Livaudais smiled a little, and lifted his chin and indicated in the direction of the door behind them. "The board knew they couldn't do that like that. They were in a panic trying to figure out how to end that sit-in, especially once they made the asinine decision to close the schools over it, and they knew the kids would listen to me. So I made a deal."

Gray and Doreen sat down in two seats across from Dr. Livaudais's desk. "What sort of deal?" Doreen asked.

"I get the kids to end their occupation at the high school. That was easy. I just told the students that if they ended it I would get my job back. So now I have my job back, at least until my contract runs out in June. I also made them give me the final say on any discipline of the students involved in the protests." Dr. Livaudais turned his gaze from Doreen to Joe.

"Yes, sir," Joe said.

"What's this about drinking?" Gray asked Dr. Livaudais.

"That's what I want to know, Mr. Alsobrook. Now, Joe, you know I appreciate the way you've stood up the last couple weeks, but if you were drinking on school grounds, I can't just let you off. We suspended three black kids on the track team for drinking last month, for passing a bottle of beer around on the team bus after a meet. I do nothing to you if you were drinking, and we've got a whole different set of problems. They say you were drinking grain alcohol from a mason jar?"

"It's not true, Doc. They're making it up," Joe exclaimed. He turned back to Gray. "I didn't do it, Dad. The coaches are just trying to get rid of me."

"Son, why don't you sit," Dr. Livaudais said, pointing to a chair beside the two his parents sat in. Joe sat down and stared at the edge of the superintendent's desk. "They want to expel you, which is absurd. They're overreaching, which is how I'm sure it isn't true. You've pissed them off. You're not playing by the rules they thought they knew."

Gray felt a lump rise in his throat. He moved his hand off his lap and let it rest on the arm of Joe's chair. "So what should we do, Doc?" Gray asked. "What about that other boy? I'm sure his parents aren't going to sit still for it if Joe isn't punished somehow."

"That's bullshit, Dad. I'm sorry, Doc, but he had it coming," Joe said.

"No, Joe, he didn't. What did I tell all of you when you marched over here? Stay peaceful, I told you. That's where your power is. Now you've put you and me, both, in a bind."

"But he yelled out across the parking lot so the whole school could hear. 'Nigger girl, suck my dick,' and nobody was going to say anything to him. He needed to be called out." Joe leaned into the back of the chair.

Dr. Livaudais looked at Joe for a second, made sure he was done. "Even if that's true, Joe, and even if you're the one who needed to call him out, you did more than that. Boy's parents say he has two cracked ribs."

"You can't expel my son," Doreen said. "You can't even suspend him, Dr. Livaudais. He's got scholarships lined up, and they won't give them to a discipline case. My son is not a bad kid. He's better than most of those kids at that school, and you know it. And we know it." Her voice remained calm, but Gray knew she was seething.

"Mrs. Alsobrook, I do know it. I also know cracked ribs is an awfully convenient diagnosis. I can't see the truth of that the way I can see Joe's face. Despite what those white board members think, I'm not stupid. But what I'm going to do is this. We're going to announce a three-day suspension for Joe. But it's not going on the books. Basically just stay home from school for three days, Joe. Mrs. Sewell in the library is going to gather your assignments and drop them off at your house each afternoon, and you have to get it all done. Understand?"

"Yes, sir. Thank you."

"Mrs. Alsobrook, are you good with this?" Dr. Livaudais asked.

"I don't like it. I want that other boy suspended, too, but I understand it."

Gray stood, and everyone else stood then, too.

"Doc, thank you." He reached his hand across the desk. "Whatever's going on in this town, thank you. Joe thinks real high of you, and I trust him."

Dr. Livaudais grasped Gray's hand.

THE LAST DAY of Joe's suspension was the last day of deer season. The week had already been long. The fire engine had gotten back on-line, and was followed by four pickups, three log skidders, and a forklift. They got them all back working again, and Gray took the day off.

While it was still dark, Gray slipped into his camo cover-alls and hunting boots, grabbed his thirty-thirty from the cabinet in the corner of their bedroom, and tried to pad as quietly as he could down the hall to the kitchen. He poured cereal into a bowl. When he turned from the fridge with his milk, Joe was standing there. His hair was bed-mussed, but he had on jeans and an olive green sweatshirt, a beat-up pair of hiking boots.

"Come with you?" Joe asked.

"Don't you have schoolwork to stay up with?" Gray asked.

"I'll finish it up when we come back. It's the last day of the season, ain't it?"

Gray set the milk carton down, and turned and grabbed another bowl from the cabinet. "Pour yourself some cereal, and be quick. I'll go grab you the twelve-gauge from the cabinet. Don't know if it's been cleaned recently."

"No, Dad, I'm not going to shoot. Just want to come hang out in the woods with you. I'm going to bring my camera." Gray looked at Joe, thinking about it, a day in the woods with someone who wasn't there to hunt.

"I'm glad to hang out with you, Joe, but you might get bored. We aren't going to be there to talk."

Joe poured cereal into his bowl. "I know how it goes."

An hour later, Gray and Joe sat next to each other twenty feet up in an oak tree in one of the mill's tree plantations, surrounded by medium-growth pine, probably two more years to harvest. Their legs dangled over the edge, and they leaned their backs against the trunk of the tree. Gray had two thermoses between them, one filled with coffee and the other with bourbon. He held his rifle loose across his lap, pointed down toward the ground as he slowly scanned back and forth through the green needles of the pines. Joe, too, was quiet and looking. Every now and then, Gray heard the shutter click on Joe's camera.

The camera had been Gray's, a basic K1000 he'd bought the first year they came out, in 1976. He'd taken a decade of pictures with it, children at Christmas and Easter, Lilah and Ruthie with prom dates, boys who looked too confident in their rented tuxedoes. When Joe was a freshman in high school and started showing an interest in photography, Gray gave the K1000 to Joe and moved up to a fancy Canon that never satisfied him the way his old camera did.

Gray reached down to the whiskey thermos and unscrewed the top and took a sip. The day had dawned muted and wet, a cold front coming through and reasserting itself after the previous week's freak weather. The bourbon felt good, better than the coffee. He offered the thermos to Joe.

"It's not the coffee, Dad," Joe whispered.

"Just take a small sip, then," Gray whispered back. Joe took it, and slurped from it. Gray expected Joe to cough on it, but the boy didn't even flinch as he handed the thermos back to Gray. Gray screwed the cap back on and set it down, then patted Joe on the shoulder as they both kept looking through the trees and brush.

A fluttering of wings exploded from a nearby tree and two doves took flight. Joe's camera was on them quick and he fired off four shots.

"You focused that quick?" Gray asked, startled by the sudden action such that he'd forgotten to stay quiet.

"Think so, and had my exposure right, too," Joe said back in a whisper. "Guess I'll see later when I can get them into the darkroom at school."

For the next hour, all was quiet, except for the dripping of gathered mist and dew from the trees to the ground below, the occasional metallic sound of the thermos caps unscrewing and screwing back, the breathing of the men.

As the clouds began to thin, a colder, brisker wind blew. In the brighter glare of the clearing day, Gray saw movement in the trees below, at about thirty yards. Close. He elbowed Joe and pointed in the direction of the shifting limbs. Two deer stepped into view, a medium-sized doe followed by a young buck, maybe six or seven points on his rack. They stopped and raised their noses to the air. Joe and Gray stayed still. The deer lowered their heads again, rooting through the carpet of pine needles, pulling up weeds and grass hiding underneath.

Gray raised his gun to his shoulder, sighted down the length of the barrel at the buck. Before he closed one eye, he saw Joe bring his camera up. He'd told Joe on the drive down that, if they saw any deer, he was to hold his shutter until after Gray got off a shot, to not spook the deer with the sound of the camera.

The deer continued grazing, slowly stepping closer. Gray kept the rifle trained on them until he had a clear shot, no limbs between him and them. Joe continued to hold off with his camera. Gray took a deep breath, held it. The world stopped around him, the deer coming into sharp focus. He lightly squeezed the trigger.

But another shot went off from the other side of the deer, just as Gray put the final pressure to his own trigger. The doe bolted, and the buck's legs tensed to jump after her when Gray's own rifle went off, and the buck fell, stone still, to the forest floor. Joe then got off three shots of his own, winding the film fast between shutter clicks, before Gray lowered his gun and said, "Come on, Joe, let's get down there."

Joe scrambled down the ladder first, jumping the last five feet. Gray followed, more slowly, taking the rungs all the way to the bottom so he wouldn't jar any old injuries. Last day of the season, and there would be venison in the deep-freeze after all. Tenderloins, steaks, packs of ground venison for burgers or meat sauce. Sausages. And Joe here for the kill, too.

As they quickly closed the ground to the fallen buck, they heard footfalls coming from the other direction. An older white man, a camo-patterned down coat and thick canvas camo pants, a long-barreled gun in his hand, came walking up to the deer, their deer.

"What you doing, fella?" he asked, not nicely.

"Getting ready to take care of my kill," Gray said. "You having any luck today?"

"Ain't your kill, mister. I just shot him from my stand over there," he said, pointing the tip of his gun up and behind him. He shifted his look over to Joe and narrowed his eyes.

"I hate to disagree with you, sir," Gray said, "but I know it was my shot that got him. Had him in my sights for ten seconds, and squeezed down careful on him. Look," Gray said, easing with the toe of his boot at a dark hole in the upper right flank of the fallen buck, red blood pumping from it. "That's where my shot went in."

"What're you even doing in these woods? It's my brother's land," the man said. He raised the point of his gun up ever slightly, not exactly pointing it at Joe and Gray.

"We have a misunderstanding, then, mister, because this is my company's land, and that stand over there is the stand I've hunted from for ten years," Gray said, dropping a layer of civility from his voice.

The man looked in doubt for a second, his bluff called, then he looked back at Joe's face, then down at the camera gripped in his hands. "Boy, what you doing out here with that thing?"

"Sir, it's my camera, but I know good enough about hunting, and I've killed deer before, if that's what you're getting at," Joe said.

"Now Joe, don't be impolite," Gray said.

"Sorry, Daddy. You know, that's clearly a thirty-thirty wound in that deer, and this man's got a twelve-gauge. Maybe he put a load of shot into that doe, but he didn't drop this buck."

The man's gun lowered an inch, and he took a step back. "Smart boy," he spat. Gray knew he likely wanted to say "smart ass" but had the sense not to.

"That's right, he is a smart boy," Gray said. "Your doe ran off that way," he added, pointing off into the brush.

The man didn't move to walk away yet, though.

He stared at Joe's face again. "Boy, don't I know you?"

"No, sir, I don't think so," Joe said.

"I've seen you in the papers or something?"

"You don't know my son," Gray said. "Now you get on, and I won't report you for poaching on mill land."

The man sneered, an ugly smile, mean, crooked across his face. "That's it," he said, still looking at Joe. "You're that nigger-loving kid. I know I've seen you. And you," he said to Gray, "raising nigger-loving kids. You can keep your piss-poor little six-pointer." He turned and walked back into the woods. "Shit," he said as he retreated.

A COUPLE DAYS LATER was Sunday again. Gray rolled out of bed and headed to the Pancake House for the first time in two weeks. A thin casing of ice cloaked every pine needle and shined from the low spots in the gutters along the road, as if winter had never left.

All the old men were already gathered around the table when Gray pulled up his chair and turned a coffee cup over. "And *damn* if them azaleas didn't all bloom and then freeze for sure," Bill was saying. "Linda's having a fit. Says I'm going to have to dig them all up and plant new ones in the spring."

Blaine had eyed Gray as he sat down, but turned back to Bill. "Didn't you just do that a couple years ago, Bill?" he asked.

"Shit don't change," Gray interrupted. "Shit don't never change."

Most of the old men shook their heads and murmured agreement, all except for Blaine. He turned back to Gray. "That what you really believe, Gray? That what you're teaching your kid?"

In that moment of direct confrontation, finally, the polite insinuating dropped, Gray felt clarity. Maybe it was the incident with the older man in the woods a couple days before, but Gray no longer felt squeamish or unsure about how or whether to push back against Blaine or against any of them. "Tell you what, Blaine," Gray said evenly, "Joe thinks for himself. That's what I guess I taught him. You may not like it. Hell, sometimes maybe even I may not like it, but at least he ain't going around yelling 'faggot' and 'nigger' all over this town like, well, like some of the kids are."

Blaine slid his chair back on the linoleum, stood and leaned over the table toward Gray, his jaw clenched tight, his eyes peering out from under his eyebrows, like he was ready to shoot fire from them. "Now you just better watch ...," he began, loudly.

"Mr. Cranston," said Glinda, the waitress, coming from around the counter with the coffee pot and touching him lightly on the elbow, "it ain't time for y'all to be going yet. Have some fresh coffee in your cup." She guided him back down into his seat and poured the coffee, sneaking a look up at Gray as she did so.

When she left the table, Blaine said, more quietly this time, calmly, "You need to watch yourself, Gray. This town's got a long memory."

Gray thought about that for a moment. He thought about all the towns he'd marched through in foreign lands in the Army, and about all the base towns he'd lived in. He thought about the little Arkansas town his father had left him and his mom in. Then he sighed and turned his hands up. "Well, Blaine, I reckon I know all that. But, you know, it's my town, just like it's your town and these boys' town here around this table, and Glinda's town, too. I don't know what else to do about it. When the azaleas die, we plant some new ones, I guess."

Blaine grunted, and that was the last the grumpy bastards of the Pancake House had to say about the school protests of 1990.

THE NIGHT JOE GRADUATED from Meadowview High School a couple months later, Gray was sitting in the stands at the Memorial Stadium watching the kids walk across the stage. When Joe got his diploma, Gray let out a long sigh of relief. Joe had been looking forward to getting his paper from Dr. Livaudais, a role the superintendent filled every year, but two weeks before the ceremony Dr. Livaudais packed up his office and left for a school district two counties over.

Seemed that the deal to reopen the schools and reverse his firing earlier in the year was just the beginning of the negotiations between Dr. Livaudais and the white Board members—the black Board members having never returned from their walk-out—as Dr. Livaudais had held a discrimination lawsuit over their heads until they agreed to a buy-out as long as he left town quietly.

So, instead of giving Dr. Livaudais a hug up on that stage, one last public poke in the eye to the folks in the town, Joe had quietly taken his diploma from the white president of the School Board, a grim look on Joe's face but nothing further. Gray had thought Joe might flip off the Board president, or maybe the whole audience, or refused to take the stage, start a sit-in, or just walk out, leaving his name being called out with a conspicuous non-response and an echo against the concrete stadium stands. Instead, Joe seemed, almost, like all the other kids, done. Just done, and nothing more.

The next morning, for once on a Saturday Gray figured he would let Joe sleep and would cut the grass and straighten up the yard himself. But as Gray was putting his coffee cup into the sink Joe walked into the kitchen in shorts and a ratty, grass-stained t-shirt.

"Hey," Gray said. "Didn't expect you to be up and around this morning."

"It was an early night. Not much of a place for me around here anymore."

"What do you mean?"

"Let's just say I didn't feel too welcome at anyone's gatherings last night. I just need to survive the summer, Daddy, then I'm gone from here." Joe looked Gray steadily in the eye as he said this, and Gray's heart broke a little.

"You've got your family here, Joe, so it ain't as bad as all that."

"And what's up with that?" Joe asked. "I mean, we're not even from here—you and Mom, y'all come from somewhere else. Lilah and Ruth weren't even born here. I'm the only one can say he was born and raised in this place, and I don't want nothing to do with it." Joe sat down on a stool at the counter.

Gray leaned back against the sink. He paused until Joe looked down at the counter in front of him. "It's not that easy, Joe, not any part of what you just said."

Without looking up, Joe almost mumbled, "It's just, it's not what I ever thought it would come to."

"It never is," Gray said.

"You can't make a difference in a place like this."

"You don't know you haven't made a difference, son, to somebody. You just got to live your life. Maybe you're right. Maybe you can't do it here. You've got that choice."

"Damn right," Joe said, peeking up at Gray and then looking back at the counter.

"But I've got that choice, too, and so does your Mama. A long time ago we chose to not keep moving around, to make a place our own. So you go off and find your consequences in college or somewhere else, but we're here. Here's where you'll find us."

Joe said nothing, but Gray could tell he was thinking over what he'd said. He watched as Joe cracked his knuckles, shifted on the stool, then Gray told him, "Alsobrooks don't run. We stay where we're rooted."

Joe stood and took a step toward Gray. They looked each other eye to eye, Joe as tall as his father now. They stood relaxed. Morning light came in through the window over the sink. It might be hot that day, but they were used to it.

"I understand all that, Dad," Joe said, "but it isn't for me, these roots in this place. You've got to know that."

"I get it, Joe." He put a hand on Joe's shoulder. "Come on. Let's get out there and get to work."

Tad Bartlett received his undergraduate degrees in theater and creative writing from Spring Hill College in Mobile, Alabama; a JD from Tulane University; and, to make up for the law degree, an MFA from the Creative Writing Workshop at the University of New Orleans. He is a founding member of the Peauxdunque Writers Alliance and the Managing Editor of the Peauxdunque Review. His creative non-fiction has been named a "notable" essay by Best American Essays, and has appeared in The Chautauqua Literary Journal, The Bitter Southerner, and the online Oxford American. His fiction has been published by The Baltimore Review, Carolina Quarterly, Stockholm Review of Literature, Bird's Thumb, and others. He lives in New Orleans with his wife and three children. Tad Bartlett on the web: https://wp.me/P1NwPI-A

Thank you to the Wapshott Press sponsors, supporters, and Friends of the Wapshott Press.

Muna Deriane

Kathleen Warner

Rachel Livingston

James and Rebecca White

Debbie Jones

Steven Acker

Ann Siemens

Suzanne Siegel

Aubrey Hicks

Carol Colin

Ted Waltz

Kathleen Bonagofsky

Cynthia Henderson

Nancy Lilly

Jeff Morawetz

Patricia Nerad

Amanda Nerad

Elaine Padilla

Laurel Sutton

Deana Swart

The Wapshott Press is a 501(c)(3) not-for-profit enterprise publishing work by emerging and established authors and artists. We publish books that should be published. We are very grateful to the people who believe in our plans and goals, as well as our hopes and dreams. Our new website is at www. WapshottPress.org. Donations gratefully accepted at WapshottPress.net.

www.ingramcontent.com/pod-product-compliance
Lightning Source LLC
Chambersburg PA
CBHW070534130626
46555CB00003B/1409